FIC   Lewis, Stephen C.

        The monkey rope.

$18.95

DATE			

The Monkey Rope

The Monkey Rope

Stephen Lewis

Walker & Co.
New York

Fic

First published in the United States of America in 1990
by Walker Publishing Company, Inc.
Published simultaneously in Canada by Thomas Allen & Son
Canada, Limited, Markham, Ontario
Library of Congress Cataloging-in-Publication Data
Stephen C. Lewis
The Monkey rope / Stephen Lewis
ISBN 0-8027-5761-8
I. Title.
PS3562.E9755M66 1990
813'.54—dc20   89-25108
CIP

Printed in the United States of America
2 4 6 8 10 9 7 5 3 1

TO CAROLYN

for her loving support
and more, her intelligent criticism

THE MONKEY ROPE

. . . from the ship's steep side, did I hold Queequeg down there in the sea, by what is technically called in the fishery a monkey-rope, attached to a strong strip of canvas belted round his waist....and should poor Queequeg sink to rise no more, then both usage and honor demanded, that instead of cutting the cord, it should drag me down in his wake.

. . . Nor could I possibly forget that, do what I would, I only had the management of one end of it.

Melville, *Moby Dick*,
Chapter LXXII,
"The Monkey-rope"

▽

One

SEYMOUR LIPP SURVEYED HIS desk again and then buzzed his secretary on the intercom. While he waited, he tore the top sheet from the legal pad on which he had been jotting notes on the Kaiser case and crumpled the paper into a firm wad. He took aim and spun the paper ball with backspin toward the wastepaper basket. The ball caught the rim of the basket, hung for a second, and then dropped in. He imagined the roar of the crowd as he prepared for another attempt, but from the corner of his eye he spotted his secretary.

Tall and angular, Dorothy Wilson stopped in the doorway to Seymour's cubicle. She was all spindly legs and arms, and today, dressed in a green dress, she looked, to Seymour, like a giant, but benevolent, grasshopper. She had removed her horn-rimmed glasses, and she twirled them in one hand while she smoothed a wisp of her severely cut gray hair with the other.

"Where's the Kaiser file, Dorothy?" he asked. "I know I left it on top, right here, so I could get to it first thing this morning." He drummed his fingers on the place where he had last seen the folder.

She reddened slightly.

1

"Mr. Brown was in early and took the file. He said you were too distracted, with your father in the hospital and all, and he was giving it to Birnhauser. I'm sorry." She put her glasses on again, and stepped closer to Seymour's desk. "I said you were working on the case, that you were almost finished, but he just gave me that iceman smile of his and walked off with it."

Seymour sank back into his chair, his fingers still running over his papers as though he expected the file to materialize.

"That's okay," he said. "It was bound to happen sooner or later." He started to smile, but his anger flashed. "Jesus . . . Birnhauser, of all people."

"I know," Dorothy said. "I thought the same thing. It's just not fair. What are you going to do?"

Seymour picked up a sheaf of notes on the case, crumpled it into a ball, and tossed it to Dorothy.

"I guess I'll have to find out how bad it is." He reached for the telephone, but Dorothy placed her hand on his. It was surprisingly warm.

"He's tied up all day. I made an appointment for you for after lunch tomorrow."

"Thanks," Seymour said. "There's nothing like waiting for the other shoe to drop."

Dorothy moved toward the doorway, and then stopped.

"Maybe it won't. I hope not. It's taken me a long time to train you. I don't know if I have the patience to deal with another young lawyer, fresh out of school." As she turned to leave the office, she banked the paper ball off the wall and into the basket.

It hadn't taken Seymour long to realize that he would never make partner at Klemmer, Schotelheim, and Brown, but he did not want to be forced out. Klemmer had died the year before Seymour joined the firm, but he still remembered his mentor, Schotelheim, an imposing man, even in his seventies, just a little stoop to his shoulders, his hair and mustache full and snow white, his voice a marvel of resonance. He would come to the office at ten o'clock each day, his newspaper folded under his arm, his overcoat wrinkled, and his shoes needing a shine. The rumor in the office was that he still did his own research, and Seymour could believe that he would. Because Schotelheim had personally interviewed and hired him, they developed a special relationship. Seymour had often come to Schotelheim with a jumble of details on his note pads looking to him like a pile of a child's pick-up sticks, all intersecting lines pointing in different directions. The old attorney, however, could find the important junctures of fact and law at a glance, and brush aside the rest. Seymour came to depend upon these sessions, but one day Schotelheim walked in with no newspaper and stayed just long enough to announce his retirement.

That left Brown, the young and aggressive senior partner from Dallas, to run the business. Brown was perhaps as brilliant as Schotelheim, although Seymour would not yet concede that point, but his bright blue eyes were cold. On first meeting Seymour he had measured his worn tweed jacket and wrinkled trousers, now a little shabby and strained by the ten or fifteen pounds he had recently gained, paused at the fresh shirt and the new striped tie his mother had insisted he buy only at the discount store off Atlantic Avenue, and then held Seymour's attention for a full minute before extending his hand. Seymour had tried to look past him to Schotelheim, but the old lawyer had disappeared into the corridor.

Seymour sat at his desk studying his handwritten résumé when Dorothy dropped the thick folder for the Kaiser case, bulging with the effluvium of a contested inheritance in front of him.

"I don't know how this got here," she said.

Seymour looked up at her and smiled. He noticed that her

blue eyes, usually watery and dull, now sparkled.

"Thanks," he said simply. He searched for something to say that would respond to the energy in her face, but she dismissed further comment with a wave of her hand.

"Just put that other away, at least for now. I'll type it up for you when," she paused, "and if, you need it."

He slipped the résumé into the top drawer, and started sorting through the correspondence and depositions in the folder. His mind, though, kept running back to his father in his hospital bed. Mr. Lipp would not, he knew, leave such a tangled mess as this. His father was no Horace Kaiser, a wealthy importer, who had died two months ago, leaving an ex-wife and grown children from one marriage, and a current, much younger wife to whom he had willed the bulk of his estate. Seymour's firm had handled the man's business dealings, and now it represented the first wife, who was contesting the will, which had been offered for probate, claiming that the man had not been competent to write a new will, and that he had been unduly influenced by his wife who had kept him shut away from his friends and family. The old man, the ex-wife had told Seymour, had probably died trying to keep the whore happy, and who was she kidding, she had been sleeping around plenty, the old bastard could hardly get it up. I should know, she had said, believe me, I should know.

The new will, drawn up only a month before the man died, seemed to mention assets of which the testator wanted to dispose, but which he no longer possessed. The narrow parameters of the case did not concern Seymour as much as they should, he knew. He wondered instead how to determine the rights of the first wife whose flesh had first been wed to the man, and who had, at least on occasion, been one with him, against the claim of the second, who had extracted him from the dead pod of a relationship and comforted him in his failing health. These were questions worthy of the rabbis, who argued Talmud in the faded print hanging on his dinette wall, he thought, and maybe tonight as he sat at his table, one of them would raise his thumb in an exhilarated demonstration of his answer.

A cough broke into his thoughts, and he looked up to see Dorothy standing before his desk.

"Mr. Brown would like to see you right away."

"Well, Dorothy," he said, "it's been nice. Do me a favor though, will you?"

She nodded.

"When I'm gone, would you incinerate my nameplate in front of the building, at precisely five o'clock, just as Birnhauser stumbles out the door?"

"I'll do better than that," she replied. "I'll buy you a drink at O'Neill's and we can use it for a swizzle stick."

"Swizzle stick. I like that. It sounds right."

The corridor was lined with the cubicles of the junior attorneys, and each of them watched through the glass panels of his door as Seymour passed. Their names were displayed on strips slid into holders. Birnhauser, a nephew of Schotelheim, used to have the spot closest to Brown, but he had been eased back down the hall toward the computer room, which occupied a large open area to the side of the partners' corridor. Seymour paused by Birnhauser's door and knocked on the glass. Birnhauser looked up and smiled, his florid face still handsome. He had the same good looks he'd had in his Princeton days, but now the boyish charm of the eyes had turned sour and the slip of hair flirting with his brows was gray. Seymour decided he could still like Birnhauser, even if he looked like an overgrown preppie, even forgive the fact that he had, however unwittingly, stolen the Kaiser case from him.

Brown's name was painted in large block letters in gold leaf on his solid oak door. The contrast with the associates' glass and temporary nameplates was sharp. And intentional, Seymour had concluded. Seymour traced the letters on the nameplate, straightened his tie, and knocked on the door.

Brown's secretary was about twenty-five, cool, and rigidly professional. She ran her finger down the appointment calendar and found Seymour's name. Her fingernails were long and carefully manicured, and Seymour noticed that there was no keyboard on her desk. She pushed an intercom button on her phone, and the door to Brown's private office swung open.

"Mr. Lipp is here to see you," she said needlessly.

Seymour rose and turned to face the imposing figure of the senior partner. Brown shook his hand before leading him by the shoulder to a seat in front of the large desk that dominated his office. As the door began to shut behind them Seymour turned and caught a glimpse of the secretary. She glanced at her watch and entered a check on the calendar. At least, Seymour thought, the pain can't last too long, only until the person owning the next name appears. He turned his attention to Brown who had walked to a cabinet behind his desk.

"What'll you have?" he asked.

"Scotch, on the rocks. I like to keep things simple."

Disapproval flickered beneath Brown's fixed smile. He was a tall man, once lean but now somewhat beefy, a wide receiver in his college days at SMU, good enough to consider, and then reject, a professional career. He poured a couple of inches of Glenlivet into two glasses, and plopped into each glass two miniature ice cubes from a tray beneath the sink. He handed the drink to Seymour, and they both raised their glasses to their lips.

"Here's to simplicity," Brown said.

Seymour felt the scotch slide down his throat.

"Very good. Very smooth."

Brown twirled his glass so that the ice clinked.

"Lipp, I'll get right to the point. I apologize for not having the opportunity to be frank with you earlier. The other day

when your secretary called, I didn't have time to talk to you."
He paused. "And I do not like to conduct such conversations
on the phone."

"I can appreciate that," Seymour said. He took a deep
swallow, and flushed. His anxiety yielded before a rush of
hostility, but his nerves pulled his lips back from his teeth
into a smile.

"Yes, well we'll see," Brown said. "I am concerned because
I do not want to lose this Kaiser case, and I don't think we
should. That's why I turned it over to Birnhauser, because
of his experience."

Seymour could not resist the impulse.

"I don't know that I need the help."

Brown's lips quivered for a moment and then relaxed.

"Lipp, don't underestimate Birnhauser. He's a damned
good lawyer. And he knows the kind of people our clients
are, what their interests are."

Seymour bristled. "Meaning?" he asked.

"Don't get cute with me, now," Brown drawled. "You
know exactly what I mean. Whatever else you may be, you're
not stupid." He picked up a folder from his desk and
skimmed over it. "Peace Corp, Public Defender, not our
usual credentials, but we had hopes for you, or at least the
old man did. And I agreed. I thought it was in the firm's best
interest to hire the best talent, whatever the background,
and not only rely on the usual prestige schools that produce
people like Birnhauser.

"But for some time I've been thinking that maybe I was
wrong, that maybe you could not escape your background."
He picked up a document from his desk, ran his eyes up and
down the first page, and then handed it to Seymour.

"Do you recognize this?" he asked.

"Of course. It is the draft memorandum on the Kaiser case
I prepared."

"Exactly. And that is what I want to discuss with you."

"Sir?" Seymour waited for the partner to continue.

"It reads like a novel, complete with plot and character motivation. Interesting, well done. But," he paused, "absolutely useless." He tossed the memorandum back onto his desk and wheeled to face Seymour.

"Tell me," he demanded, "why did you choose corporate law, when your talents seem to lie elsewhere."

The question stung, Seymour realized, because it was precisely the one he had asked himself many times over the past few months. He tried to deflect it.

"When I stopped growing at 5'10", I realized I wasn't going to make the Knicks, so I went to law school and bounced around, as you have indicated. When I came back to New York from California, I came here looking for Mr. Green."

Brown permitted himself a sarcastic twitch of the lips and then his face darkened, as he picked up the memorandum again. "There are many ways to make money. But let's talk about this. Mrs. Kaiser was on the phone a little earlier to ask what was happening, and I told her that I would have to check with you and Birnhauser. I was going to talk to you before she called. Mrs. Kaiser is a very important client, even since her husband's death." He flipped to a page in the memorandum. "I really don't know what your problem is. It seems clear from the depositions that the new will won't stand up. What about this painting, the one he wants his second wife's daughter to have because she always admired it? That's the woman's testimony, anyway."

"Yes, I know," Seymour said. "The painting had been promised to his own daughter in the old will. But really, is that the issue, when we're talking of an estate worth upwards of a hundred million? One lousy painting? And it is lousy, second-rate."

Brown raised his eyebrows.

"And are you now an art critic, or appraiser? Really, Lipp,

you trouble me. But the point is that the old man, on his death bed, was obviously coerced. Don't you agree?"

"I'm not sure it's as clear as all that. The new will is a little ragged in places, but defensible."

Brown leaned his bulk toward Seymour.

"Are you talking as one who has dealt with ex-wives."

"No, sir," Seymour snapped the words. "That's history. I'm talking about the will."

"I wonder," Brown said. "You say the will is defensible. Need I remind you that it is your job to attack that will, to shred it, to grab hold of those ragged edges—such as the fact that the recipient of the painting is also an interested witness—and tear the whole thing apart so that our client, acting on behalf of her children, receives her just inheritance." He paused. "Including the painting. Even if she wants to use it as a doormat for their dirty shoes."

Seymour felt his bile rise.

"Yessir," he said, "that is our job."

"Well, let's see that we do it. I expect movement on this case by first thing next week. Have another memorandum on my desk, one that shows how we will win, not how we might lose, first thing Monday morning."

Seymour nodded, and turned to leave. Brown's eyes froze him.

"Was there anything else Mr. Brown?"'

"Yes, there is."

Seymour waited while the partner ran his long fingers through his closely cropped hair, and then walked to the bar to refill his glass. When he again faced Seymour the harshness had disappeared from his face, which was now almost sad.

"I guess the old man never spoke to you that way," he said.

His shift caught Seymour off guard.

"We had," he said, "a rather different relationship."

"Well, he's not . . ." Brown began.

"No, he's not," Seymour finished for him, "and it's a damned shame."

The message, in Dorothy's precise hand, said only that a Mrs. Constantino had called, and that she would be waiting for him in the lobby after work. "That was my landlady's name when I was a kid," he said in answer to her quizzical look. "I am sure, though, that this person could not be her."

He crumbled the note into the wastepaper basket and pressed his hands over his eyes, as though in weariness, but more to focus on the images that flashed through his mind: the terror in his father's eyes as he lay in his hospital bed, the heavyset figure of his mother stooping over the kitchen stove, and the muscular shape and sneering lips of Junior Constantino. He held that one image while he placed next to it another, when it was he lying in a different hospital bed, and Junior's face screamed silently in remorse.

Seymour sensed, as the elevator descended, that paths that had separated were now about to join. At first, it was only the name and the puzzle it offered that tightened his stomach. And then it was the anticipation that here again was somebody he had tried so hard to forget, and in the forgetting had remembered even more painfully.

The doors slid open. He was not surprised to see her sitting, legs crossed, nervously puffing a cigarette.

She had changed a great deal, but there was still that haunted look in her eyes, the sudden smile on her painted lips, and the familiar whisper of an invitation from between her thighs that drained his mouth dry.

She rose from her chair, smoothed down her shorts, and adjusted the tank top over her breasts. She smiled warmly, and her teeth still glistened as moistly white as they had done so many years ago.

"How ya doin', gimpy?"

In spite of himself, he broke into a laugh that began as a pucker on his lips and then drew the tension from his taut stomach until it exploded through his mouth.

Lois joined him for a moment, and then she pressed her fingers against his lips. She glanced over his shoulder at the doorman.

"Shh!" she murmured. "Let's go someplace where we can talk."

Seymour reached over and grabbed her arm, surprised at the firmness of her biceps. He held it for a moment, and then he saw the faint, but unmistakable traces. She pulled her arm away and held it against her side.

"Yes," she said. "But no more, not for a long time."

"Look," he said quietly, "I'd like to help you if I can."

It was not until some time later, as they sat across from each other in O'Neill's, that he realized how her sudden appearance, dressed like the hooker she probably was, and the tracks on her arm, coming right after his conversation with Brown, had made him realize that he no more belonged working for Mrs. Kaiser, with her dead husband and greedy new *shiksa* wife, than she belonged sitting in the lobby of a building that housed firms such as his own, whose business it was to help those who already had so much hold onto what they had, even in death. More than any threat from Brown, she brought him back to himself. They shared a kinship that he would never have acknowledged to the senior partner.

O'Neill's was a place of dark, scarred wood, and intimate conversations floating in the dusk of its interior. Even bright sunlight had to force its way through the thick, greenish gray glass and pierce the dusty and smoke-laden air so that the high-backed booths with their dark red leather cushions blended into shadows and smiles flashed like brief sparks from hidden faces. It was a place frequented by men who came to soften the hard edges of a day over a quiet drink, and occasionally to meet their lovers before catching the late train home to their wives and families. Seymour's blood would stir when one of these women, usually in her twenties and stylishly dressed, would slip into a booth next to a man who had been drinking alone, and when she threw her arm around the man's neck, Seymour's loneliness would turn to a palpable hurt. Birnhauser, who came only to drink, had introduced Seymour to O'Neill's, and soon, Seymour knew, he would arrive and take his usual stool at the end of the bar.

Sitting across from Lois made Seymour feel more comfortable than he had ever been in the tavern. Although he knew the other men were absorbed with their own companions, he sensed eyes caressing Lois as he steered her to a booth in the rear corner. Seymour imagined that Lois had been meeting him like this each evening, but that tonight they would find a hotel where he could wash away the dust of his arid days. He ordered drinks for them, Bloody Marys, and she smiled.

"I haven't had one of those in years," she said.

"You used to like them."

"I used to like many things." Her voice quivered, and she ground out her cigarette with considerable force. She searched his eyes.

"Seymour, I hope I'm not going to cause you to do something you'll be sorry for. I know I've caused you pain in the past, and I want you to know I wouldn't have come to you now, if I could have helped it. But we, that is, I didn't know where else to turn."

He heard, but ignored, the switch. He didn't care, at least at that moment, why she had sought him out. He wanted to tell her that he had never been able to rid his mind of her image, that there was a wildness in her that both fascinated and repelled him. He wanted to explain these paradoxical feelings to her and watch her eyes catch and magnify the light of the candle on their table, but he felt struck dumb.

"Look," he forced himself to say after a while, "I'll try to explain it to you. You've got nothing to blame yourself for. Then or now. In fact, seeing you has helped me make a decision. I'm thinking of leaving the corporate tomb, although I really don't have anything better lined up right now." He paused, "And there's my father in the hospital." She reached across the table and grasped his hand.

"Woa, counselor, you're going too fast. We have a lot of ground to cover from when we used to drink these on the couch, listening for the click of my mother's key in the lock." She lifted her drink, blood red in the candlelight. "From then until now."

From the moment he had realized who she was, he had felt suddenly liberated, and now, as the vodka made his mind spin, he forced his shoe off underneath the table, leaned back, and brought his foot up between her thighs. She shifted her weight on her chair until the blunt end of his shortened foot pressed hard against her warmth. She closed her eyes for a moment, and when she opened them her face relaxed into a comfortable glow. Seymour began to speak, but she reached across the table and brushed her fingers across his lips.

"Let me just remember for a minute," she said. She held his eyes with hers and tightened her thighs. Then she clasped his foot with both hands before pushing it away from her.

She lit a cigarette as though to confirm that they would deal with the present.

"Tell me about your father."

Seymour shrugged.

"A stroke. He's getting better. Slowly."

She held his hand, and then ran her fingers up to his neck, her touch warm and gentle. She seemed lost in thought.

"And you? What have you been doing all these years except messing up your career?"

He smiled.

"Messing up a marriage."

She lifted her eyebrows.

"Anyone I know?"

"I don't think so. I found somebody from the other side of town. Anyway, she's in California now. With our son." He spoke the words easily, but the hurt and anger rose anyway. "It's been two and a half years. I don't really know what the kid looks like anymore."

"I see, baby," she said, her eyes half closed, and her voice quiet. "Some other time, we can go over all that. I'm sorry about your father."

"Aren't you curious," she asked after a awhile, "about my name?"

His face darkened. He had not wanted to discover that secret just yet.

"It's not, I suppose, because you thought I would recognize that name, and not your own."

She shook her head.

"And you're not the one in trouble. Am I right?"

She stared down at the table, twirled the cubes in her drink, and nodded.

"Bingo!" he exclaimed. "Do I get a prize?"

"You don't have to get nasty. Look, I'm sorry, but Junior needs help, and he asked me to find you. That's what this whole charade is about."

"I knew it," he said slowly. "I knew sooner or later this would happen, at least in some shape or form. And it shouldn't surprise me that you are the messenger. I had let myself hope, you know . . ."

"Yes, I do know. And that part is also true. Please believe me."

He shook his head. "And are you also now his wife?"

She flashed a smile, and her tone became playful again. "We're not that formal about these things. You should have guessed that as well."

The day had become overcast, and the gloom darkened

inside the bar. But Seymour felt closer to her, as though they had been shut away from the world. She searched his eyes and seemed to find a different question.

"Don't you want to know about Rosalie?" she asked with a suddenly bright smile. "Now that you're a free man. Maybe you should get back together with her, get yourself a good Italian girl, from the old neighborhood."

He started to rise to the bait, but caught himself.

"I didn't even know that you would have any idea about her, and besides I haven't thought about her in years."

She reached across the table to touch his cheek. "I don't think that is entirely true."

"Maybe not," he admitted.

He settled back further in the booth. In the quiet of the place, with just the murmur of subdued conversation, and the occasional clink of glasses, he had fooled himself into thinking that she could be his for a little while without suffering the shadow of Junior and the past, but thinking about Rosalie forced him to remember the images of that time: the pure companion of his youth and the siren, neither of whom he had possessed, nor could—both inaccessible in their abstraction, and he unable to dispel either ikon.

Lois took out a cigarette and searched for a match. She fished a crumpled book out of the pocket of her shorts, and lifted the cover.

"I guess it's going to be that kind of day," she said, showing Seymour the empty book. He picked up the candle and reached across the table.

"Thanks. Why didn't I think of that? I guess that's why you're the lawyer." She inhaled deeply.

Seymour pulled a full book of matches from his pocket, and handed it to her. "I could have given you these. But I liked the candle idea. Saw it in a movie once."

"Just like you. I'm sure you spend too much damned time in movies, alone. Am I right?"

He nodded.

"Anyway," she said, "Rosalie, she's a librarian, now, after going to school at night and working as a waitress in a diner in Sheepshead Bay. You should look her up."

"That's not what I want to hear," Seymour snapped.

"Why she became a librarian, you mean? I couldn't tell you. Maybe she never recovered from the way you broke her heart." Her smile now was evil. "Or the college she went to. You know she dropped out after the first year, but she never lived at home again."

"No, none of that. I knew some of the story anyway." He lit a cigarette for himself with the candle. "What I mean is, that while I'm sitting here with you, I don't want to be talking about Junior. Or his sister. Anyway, when did you start playing matchmaker?"

He was unprepared for the violent burst of laughter that exploded from her.

"Matchmaker! Me! That's a good one! I'll have to tell him about that one. He'll get a good laugh. And his sister and you no less."

The late afternoon crowd began to arrive, their clothes soaked from a brief thunderstorm that now provided a background to their conversation. Seymour saw Birnhauser stroll in, shake himself off, and settle into his seat. Wordlessly, the bartender slid a glass in front of him. Lois followed Seymour's eyes, and her face hardened.

"I think it's stopped raining, and I should be getting you home." She leaned across the table and exhaled a warm ring of smoke. Seymour felt her hand run up his thigh. He covered her fingers for a moment, pressing them into his flesh.

"I want to spend the night with you," he said.

She smiled, "Maybe you will." She drew back. "But first there is Junior."

Lois waited outside the booth while he dialed. He heard the phone ring six or seven times before his mother picked it up.

"Mom, I won't be able to make it tonight. Something has come up." He began to turn his back to Lois, but she motioned that she would be waiting outside. On the other end of the phone line, his mother's voice was plaintive. He half listened to the litany of accusations and then told her he would see her next week when his father would be home from the hospital.

He found Lois waiting in a cab parked by the curb outside the bar.

"Everything alright?" she asked.

"Sure, just fine."

"Did you send them my regards?"

He didn't respond, and she looked hurt.

"I was serious," she insisted.

He took her measure. "Maybe next time," he said.

Sitting beside her in the back seat, Seymour tried to clear away the curtain that the vodka and scotch had draped over his mind. He leaned back and watched the sun dip toward the blackening waters of the East River beneath the Brooklyn Bridge. The solid yet graceful pillars were bathed in the red sunset, glowing an unreal pink against the gray sky. The cab crawled along, one in an antlike procession. He didn't know exactly where they were going, and he didn't care, for the moment. He would find out soon enough, and in the meantime, he was content to sit with her in silence. He noticed, though, that she became increasingly nervous, puffing deeply on her cigarette, as the cab began to work its way down Flatbush Avenue.

"What's the matter?" he asked.

"I haven't told you everything."

"I know. Don't. Let me find out one step at a time."

She smiled a little too quickly, drew his head to her, and kissed his lips. Her tongue jumped into his mouth, and he pulled her into his arms. She moved against him so that her breasts were cushioned against his chest.

He cupped her breast softly with his palm, partly to savor the anticipation, and partly because he feared that the moment would be spoiled, that they were only figures in a long suppressed dream which would vanish with the first sudden and conscious movement. He did not know if he desired the actuality, but he ached pleasantly, and so he stroked the underside of her breast with just the tips of his fingers. She murmured deep in her throat and pushed herself against his hand.

Her movement forced him to realize the present, and he felt himself begin to harden. He abandoned the dream against the thrust of her tongue and the touch of her hand between his thighs. She pulled her mouth away from his lips and drew her tongue over his neck and, moistly, behind his ear.

"I want you tonight," he said.

"And what I want," she whispered, "is to get you so hard you ache, and then when you are good and ready, let you pick a hole, and come inside me, somewhere, anywhere, but inside me."

He caught his breath and leaned against her, dimly aware of the lurch of the cab and the labored groan of its engine as it accelerated from a light. In a rush, he was with her again on the couch in her parent's apartment, performing her cruel ritual, baring the stump of his foot for her pleasure, but he did not care, he would gladly have offered himself again, right there on the cracked seat of the cab as the evening fell around them, and the driver lit a cigarette and stared straight ahead at the shimmering pattern of red lights.

She pulled back after a while as though she had read his thoughts.

"Don't let me do this to you. I'm professional now, anyway. You know that."

The words ripped through his desire, through his memory

of those long afternoons, and through his rising excitement. He moved away from her.

"I'm sorry." She sighed. "That seems to be all I can ever say to you. But I really do love you, a little, after all, and in my own way. I just wanted to tell you, so you would know. I don't want to use you. It's enough that I'm bringing you to Junior. More than enough."

The name merged the past with the present, and he withdrew to his side of the cab. He lit a cigarette and stared out the window at the line of cars approaching on the other side of the bridge. But his mind refused to be deterred and it raced back twenty years to a street in Brooklyn, the street before the house in which his family rented the second floor from the Constantinos. It was the night of July Fourth, and the black sky above the towering maples was encrimsoned and ablaze with exploding rockets and roman candles. He felt again the squeeze of Rosalie's fingers on his arm as they stood alone in the shadows, but he pulled himself free and joined the tight circle of his friends around Junior, who tossed innocent ladyfingers at their feet in a game of chicken. He saw now in the glare of the oncoming headlights the fire in Junior's eyes and his thick hand reaching into his pocket to emerge holding the fat cherry bomb, the long fingers lighting another match, but the eyes never leaving his. Then the rounded shape rolling lazily toward his feet, and too late Junior's body hurled against his in a brutal and futile shove, as the explosion reverberated even now in the quiet cab where only the click of the meter and the wheeze of the driver disturbed the silence. But there was no pain, just the torn canvas of his sneaker and the bright red blood and the shards of bone and flesh.

He felt Lois' body press against his. She leaned her head on his shoulder.

"Maybe we should just forget the whole thing," she said, her voice a whisper.

He turned to her.

"Is that what you want?"

She shook her head.

"What I said about tonight, I meant it, if you still want me."

He fought the push of his blood, and did not answer.

They rode in silence for almost an hour. The cabbie, whose hacking breaths rose in counterpoint to the steady ticking of the meter, glanced at them in his oversized rear-view mirror and then lit another cigarette.

Seymour's mind darted back and forth between the woman leaning against him like a sweetheart and the memory of her as the seductress of his youth. He made himself remember the time he had decided to buy her love, how he had been inspired by her comment one afternoon, as she circled his flesh with her warm fingers, that she had seen a pearl ring in the window of a jewelry store, and that, as she had brought her lips closer to him and whispered, the color of the pearl was just like the color of his come. He had found the ring the next day, and for some reason he had never understood, he told Junior he wanted to get it for her. He tried to erase the next scene that forced its way into his mind, but he heard again Junior's taunt that if he were a man he would just get it. His own foolish retort echoed in his memory, and then he remembered the shattering of glass, the alarm, and the sirens, and the moment of aching clarity when Junior had stared down at his foot and snarled, "Now, we're gonna be even, you bastard." And the last image of Junior hurling himself at the running policemen while he fled down an alley, pausing only to toss the ring into a garbage can.

He turned to her, and she lifted her heavy lidded eyes to him.

"Do you know why Junior got sent away the first time?" he asked.

Her eyes showed interest, but she shrugged.

"Just that he got caught breaking into a store."

"And that's all?"

She nodded.

"I was just thinking," he said, "that I saw him right before he got caught, and that was the last time. Until now."

They had just begun their slow turning on the traffic circle at Grand Army Plaza. The cab followed the circle around the grandiose monument to the soldiers of the Civil War. The huge public library, in whose quiet rooms he had spent hundreds of evenings studying, which now was home to as many homeless as scholars, stood to the left. Around the circle, and on the right, as they began their arc, was the entrance to Prospect Park. He thought the cabbie might veer off into the winding roads of the park, but the car stayed in its lane until it squarely faced the library. The cabbie looked over his shoulder, started to turn the wheel, and then cursed under his breath. Seymour caught his eye as he turned again to look behind him.

"Bastard wouldn't let me in," the cabbie said, and Seymour nodded.

They crawled around the circle until they reached the spot where they could angle onto Flatbush Avenue, and Seymour knew the centrifugal force of twenty years would now spin him home.

He had been right in guessing their destination, and the knowledge helped ease the full shock of stopping in front of his old house, the brick and stucco building he had thought now belonged to an entirely new generation.

He and Lois got out of the cab wordlessly. On the stoop sat a number of teenaged Blacks. He counted five, three girls and two boys, ranging in age from about twelve or thirteen to the oldest, and most sullen, a young man who looked to be almost twenty. They smiled at Lois, and then their eyes took his measure. He waited for somebody to say something, a greeting, or a curse, but they remained silent. Lois waved at them, and steered Seymour away from the stoop toward the rear of the house. They stopped before the cellar storm doors, freshly painted a bright green, and secured by a shiny padlock. She knocked three times, sharply, and then slipped a key into the lock. It clicked open and she lifted the lock free. Seymour started to help her lift the doors, but she stayed his arm.

"It's better if I go first. Wait here for me until I call for you." She descended the steep cement steps and disappeared inside. A few minutes later, she stuck her head up into the opening and beckoned him in. He made his way down the steps, and as he did, she pulled the doors down and slid a heavy wooden security bar into place. For a second, they were thrown into darkness. A heavy curtain hung across the doorway at the bottom of the steps. Lois pulled it aside and led him into the basement.

The first thing he noticed was how clean and attractive the place was. He had half expected to find the old furnace next to heaps of dusty coal spilled half across the cement floor, as in the days when he had lived in the house. He remembered waking up early on frigid winter mornings and listening for the clang of coal against steel as Mr. Constantino stoked the furnace, and then some time later, the first hiss of steam from the paint-encrusted radiator in his room rising against the chilled air. Instead, he discovered a paneled room about fifteen feet square with doors leading to the back and to one side. The room was carpeted with self-adhering tiles that, he saw, had been carefully laid. The room also held a sofa, an easy chair, and a glass and brass coffee table, all of clean, contemporary style. One wall was lined with walnut shelves that were filled with books. Lois noticed his surprise.

"What did you expect? Cages? Or mirrors and water beds?"

He smiled.

"They're in the back," she said with a forced laugh that did not hide her anxiety.

He felt like he was on a date, and that she was concerned about the impression her place made on him.

"It's very nice," he said. "I didn't know what to expect."

He tried to think of something else to add, but the scream of an infant from behind the side door drew his attention to Junior who entered the room, holding a baby, about a year old, red faced and howling, squirming against the thick arms of its father. It was stifling in the room, and the baby wore only a bedraggled plastic diaper that threatened to slide down its chubby legs as it gathered its stomach for each scream.

"I was just going to change Jennifer when I heard the knock," Junior said as though Seymour were not there.

"Here, let me take her," Lois said. Junior handed the infant to her, and the baby stopped screaming for the second that it hung, suspended, between the two adults. Then as Lois drew her to her breast, she began again. When Lois reached the door, she looked back at Junior.

"Your friend is here," she said, "just like I promised."

She brushed at her eye as she walked through the door. She cooed at her baby and rocked her in her arms, then shut the door behind her.

Junior turned to Seymour and extended both his arms. He was a tall, muscular man with straight, luxuriously thick and shiny black hair that he let grow long enough to cover his ears and reach almost to the base of his neck. When he walked, his hair swung away from his ear and revealed a diamond stud. Both arms bore tattoos, a snake clutched in the claws of an eagle on one, and the words "Do It!" on the other. His eyes flashed intensely, like highly burnished slivers of steel. He wore jeans with a thick black belt buckled on the side, and a sleeveless undershirt, and his thick chest hair spilled over the top. His hands looked gnarled as if they had been crushed and inexpertly set, though oddly, the fingers were long and almost delicate.

He grabbed Seymour's hand and squeezed it just hard enough to cause a twinge of pain, and then he drew him to his chest and embraced him.

Seymour looked toward the door behind which Lois had disappeared, but it remained closed. He felt trapped and abandoned, shocked into sobriety, wondering why he was in this room with this man, wondering and yet knowing that his life had permitted him no other choice, and that this meeting would have to be in this place. It was as certain as his sure knowledge that Junior had not changed, he had only become more subtle. Instead of the cherry bomb, it would be a request to do something significant, something he would have to stomach, however, unhappily, to pay his debt incurred in front of that jewelry store. He had always known that he and Junior had not squared accounts, that quite possibly they never could.

He fixed his eyes on the belt.

"Some things haven't changed," he said.

Junior ran his fingers over the thick leather.

"Not much, anyway, but I took the studs off."

"I guess that counts as progress."

Seymour felt drawn into their shared past, and he willed himself to resist.

"Look, you figured I would come if you used Lois as bait. And you were right. You've always been right. And so I find you living just where I left you twenty years ago. Well, what the hell, what the hell is going on?"

Junior turned serious, his face now half scowl, and half an appeal for help, just like, Seymour thought, a wounded boar, savage and dangerous, but with eyes informed with a bright intelligence.

"I'll make it short and sweet. I've done time. I've hustled,

I've pimped. Yeah, don't look like that, for Lois, too, when a lot of shit was going down, and we were both pushed to the wall, but I didn't start her in the business. You, of all people, should be able to figure that out. No getting back into it was her idea. She had been retired, hadn't sold her ass in years, but we would both be strung out real bad, in bed holding on to each other to try to make the room stop spinning, and to throw the fuckin' shakes off our backs, just wanting a little time, a little relief—a little smack. We'd be too wasted to do anything but try to lie still, and she would say, 'I can get us some money,' and she wouldn't say how. I knew, and finally I said if you're gonna do that I'll get the johns, I don't want you gettin' mixed up with no perverted dude that's gonna use you until you ain't no good to nobody, and so I became," he paused, "her agent, and we did okay."

"I guess I'm supposed to congratulate you for being so good to her," Seymour said. Junior grabbed him by the shoulders and pulled him close, his eyes burning into Seymour's.

"Look, I don't need none of your wise-ass stuff. What do you know about it anyway?"

Seymour freed himself. "Nothing, you're right, I know nothing about it."

"That's right. I wouldn't let her take no spooks, or chinks, just ordinary, horny, middle-class white and bright Americans, just like you." He leered for a moment. "But forget that. It's history. Or it was until I got busted again, when we were trying to leave that all behind us, and just make it, with the baby."

"And?"

"And like I said, the pigs wouldn't let me. I got busted last week. For dealing."

"Were you?" Seymour asked. He did not know why he bothered to try this question. He had decided to believe Junior, to credit at least the urgency of his appeal. But Junior's eyes blazed.

"Do you think I'd have called you for help if I was? Do you think I'd even let you know where I lived, and how I lived? What do you think I am, anyway? If you're gonna ask stupid questions like that, you might just as well leave. I'll say good-by," he smiled, "to your old girlfriend for you."

He stepped back from Seymour and began to pace around the room. He moved slowly, his body erect and solid, tilted a little forward. Seymour felt the constrained energy and noticed the balance and sureness of the step—the walk of somebody not accustomed to making mistakes and ready to take advantage of another's weakness. He experienced again the feeling of helplessness he remembered from childhood, the sense that Junior's will was irresistible, and that this will was destructive, just as the cherry bomb had been, and it no more than an extension of the child-man who had thrown it, the explosion a realization of his energy in a moment's fury. The remorse that had followed had been a flimsy graft, fit only for a brief flowering of sympathy and then decay.

"Let's get something straight," Seymour said in a voice that cracked into a snarl. "Just let's cut the bullshit. I came here to find you again. I didn't know it would be here, but I should have known. This is where it began, and where it should end. If you're still pimping for Lois, if I'm the john in this deal, well, that's okay, too. Tell me your story, and if I can, I'll help you. We owe each other. Now, let's see what the terms are going to be."

Junior's face broadened into a smile.

"That's my man. I knew you'd come through for me. It ain't much of a story. I mean the bust was dirty. Should be easy for you to cripple. I was searched, man, with no cause. Sure, maybe I was holdin', but I don't deal, and it wasn't much anyway. They were just lookin' for me."

Seymour sat down on the sofa. He looked toward the door that led to, he supposed, their bedroom. Light seeped out from under the door, and he could hear music, some blues tune deep in bass and piano. He turned back to Junior.

"Just tell me about it." He hesitated. "I haven't had much experience with this sort of thing, lately, you know."

"It'll come back," Junior said, his face now serious. "But that's it, isn't it? Like you said, we owe each other."

$\bigtriangledown$

Two

IT HAD BEEN SO easy that Seymour felt betrayed. The terms confirmed his knowledge that the bargain struck in the explosion, and renegotiated in the pulse of red light that illuminated Junior's thick body hurled before the onrushing police, that promissory note, was now being called in by John P. O'Riley, III, an Assistant New York County District Attorney.

In a brief telephone conversation O'Riley told Seymour that he would be happy to discuss Mr. Constantino's case over lunch as soon as he was through in court. Seymour had caught up with him at the Manhattan Criminal Court, and had sat in the back of the courtroom while the prosecutor delivered his summation, demanding that the defendant, a teenaged Black man accused of selling crack to junior high students, be found guilty and locked up for as long as the law permitted.

"But your chap, now," O'Riley smiled, "is a different story."

Seymour noted the affectation, which joined the tweed cap and silk ascot, and the briar pipe. When Seymour had introduced himself to O'Riley outside the courtroom, the prosecutor had thanked him for responding so promptly to his invitation to discuss Junior's case, which they could do over lunch.

They walked to Mott Street and stopped before a store window that displayed freshly slaughtered and plucked ducks, their skins mottled in the afternoon sun. They entered a doorway that opened to stairs leading down to a tiny restaurant, no more than five or six tables in the basement of the building. They sat down at one of the bare wooden tables and ordered from a waiter whose broad smile was not diminished by the absence of front teeth.

Seymour was not prepared for amiability. From his days as a public defender, he knew of O'Riley's reputation as a headline-grabbing law-and-order advocate who often declared that the defendant he had just prosecuted had been treated too gently.

"Now, your chap," he repeated after the waiter had shuffled off to the kitchen with their order, "is quite another sort. Oh, he has a record as long as my arm, and he has done his time, but I'd hate to send him away again. It would be very unfortunate for him, seeing how he has that little baby now."

Seymour felt his guard rise. He took a sip of water and forced a smile.

"Well," he said slowly as he put the water glass down, "I'd like to see him get another chance to build a decent life for himself and for his family."

"Exactly my point," O'Riley boomed. Seymour looked around, but the other patrons seemed absorbed in their meals. O'Riley leaned across the table and lowered his voice. "You see, I too have a history of involvement with your friend. I put him away, once before, a long time ago. When he was first starting his career. But I'm sure you know all about that."

The recognition flashed through Seymour's mind, but he only set his expression into an attentive stare.

"Oh, come now," the prosecutor smiled, "don't play cat and mouse with me. I'm sure you know. The bungled robbery, a vacation at the work farm until our boy decided to shorten his stay." He sighed. "I've always regretted that one. I was too easy." O'Riley poured himself a cup of tea, sipped it, and then wiped his lips with his napkin as if to remove the memory of his weakness along with the drop of tea on his lips.

For a moment, Seymour believed that O'Riley somehow knew that it was his arm that had extended through the broken glass to snatch the ring. He felt the prosecutor's hot breath coming too close.

"History is always interesting," he said, "but let's talk about now. Your search won't hold. Nothing like probable cause. I'm going to move to dismiss."

O'Riley smiled. "Don't waste your time. You've been away too long in the corporate world."

"Do you always research opposing counsel?"

"Sometimes that's more important than precedent."

He paused while the waiter set the steamed dumplings on the table, then attacked one with practiced ease, clamping the dumpling between his chopsticks, dipping it in the duck sauce, and bringing it to his mouth.

O'Riley dabbed his mouth with his napkin. "Maybe we're getting off to a bad start here. We could prosecute, and probably make it stick. What I would like to suggest, though, is that, given the circumstances, our personal involvement with the young man, perhaps we can be a little more creative, save the taxpayers some money, and do some good at the same time."

Seymour reached for a dumpling, but it slid off his chopsticks.

"What do you have in mind?" he asked.

O'Riley smiled. "Here, let me show you. You can't squeeze the chopsticks too hard, just enough to grab it. Otherwise, it'll pop out.

"Now, what I have in mind for your friend is something like these chopsticks. I want to squeeze him, but just hard enough. And you are going to do the squeezing, if you go along with the idea."

"Meaning?"

"We'll knock the dealing charge down to possession, seventh degree, a misdemeanor, conditional sentence, no probation." O'Riley paused for effect. "And the condition is that your chap behaves himself, that you find him suitable employment, and see that he keeps his nose clean." He beamed. "Beautiful, isn't it? A new kind of reformation for the reformable, hitherto misguided young man, given a new chance under the salutary moral influence of a life-long friend, a spotlessly clean member of the community—you."

Seymour processed the rolling speech, picked out the morsels of fact. A marvelously good deal for Junior, better than could have been expected. For himself, perhaps a problem, maybe worse.

"Why all this generosity?" Seymour asked, "and why is Junior the recipient?"

O'Riley lowered his eyes as though reviewing his poker hand before offering his bet.

"It's really not all that generous, considering the revolving door our system has, regrettably, become." He picked up his chopsticks and jabbed them in front of him. "But the real point is not the revolving door, but who is going in or out." His eyes brightened. "We have to change our focus, stop beating up on the little players. They're only symptoms of the disease anyway."

"So what's new? Nobody ever claimed that Junior Constantino was major league."

"Of course. But he clutters up the system, and distracts our attention from our real mission, which is to bring the full weight of the law down on the heads of those who use people like your friend." He reached for another dumpling. "Instead of wasting my time, and that of my staff, preparing to shove Mr. Constantino into that door, we can concentrate on making a case that will stick against the head man, and believe me the door will swing only one way for him."

Seymour saw the game.

"So when do you announce your candidacy for District Attorney?" he asked.

O'Riley sat back, and brought his napkin to his lips again.

"Ah, so you see, don't you," he said slowly, "why I need your friend? And you, too. A new program is nothing without the right face."

"What makes Junior right? He's not black, after all, not your classic disadvantaged thug."

"I am making a serious proposal, counselor."

"Maybe so," Seymour said, "but you will have to accept that I am a skeptic by nature, and I don't think you've shown your hole card."

O'Riley held up his hands, and shook them over the table.

"Nothing up my sleeve." He smiled.

Seymour picked up a dumpling with his chopsticks, and then let it slide back onto the plate.

"You seem to have thought it all through. So why do you need me?"

O'Riley's eyes focused on the dumpling on Seymour's plate and the muscles in his jaw stiffened.

"Because I don't have the time to fool around, because Mr. Constantino might not regard my former kindness as kindness, might even turn me down. You are not to let that happen."

"I am his counsel, and I will make him aware of your offer." Seymour folded his napkin and stood up. "We'll take it under advisement," he said. "I'll get back to you after I speak with my client."

"Naturally. But be quick. I've scheduled a news conference for later this afternoon. And I don't want to be disappointed."

"I hope you won't say anything you'll regret. I'll talk to you as soon as I can, but I doubt it'll be before tomorrow."

O'Riley reached across the table and held Seymour's arm. "Understand me," he said. "I intend to announce this new program along with my candidacy. Don't cross me. Just sell the idea to Junior. What the hell does he have to lose?"

Seymour pulled his arm free. "You know I can't agree to anything, even if I wanted to, and that is open to serious question."

He got up and headed toward the stairs. When he turned back he saw O'Riley holding the last dumpling before his mouth.

Seymour stared out the cab window at the Bridge, but this time he was alone, and night had fallen so that the structure sparkled in a silhouette of gracefully swooping lines illuminated by thousands of twinkling lights, and the brighter glow of headlights that formed, from this distance, an almost solid yellowish white line. He lowered his eyes to the black water of the East River, drawn to its silent movement as though it would carry him to his resolution with Junior.

He knocked at the door the way Lois had done, and Junior answered almost immediately, drawing Seymour into the living room as much with the intensity of his dark eyes as with the hand that squeezed Seymour's arm. During the cab ride to Brooklyn, Seymour had considered how to describe the deal proposed by O'Riley.

Junior, though, did not give him a chance to speak.

"I don't suppose you saw the news tonight," he said, his voice quiet and controlled.

Seymour's pulse quickened. He knew he had been taken.

"No," he said. "I haven't been near a television. I met with O'Riley, and then stopped at my office to clean out some stuff. I'll be moving into my new office next week."

"Well, maybe you should look for one with a kiddie corner for me to play in." Junior smiled. "Relax man, we're all

celebrities. You, me, Lois, the baby, and that prick O'Riley."
He pointed to the phone he had ripped off the wall. "Everybody's been callin'."

"That bastard," Seymour muttered. "That son-of-a-bitch.
I knew he wouldn't wait. I should have him up on charges. He
can't do it."

Junior smiled more broadly and steered Seymour to the
couch. His eyes still blazed, but the rest of his face had
relaxed in resigned amusement.

"Hey, it ain't so bad. I've always wanted a real daddy to
look after me. Mine didn't do such a terrific job, you know."

Seymour caught his breath and forced his mind to focus.

"Let me understand this. O'Riley was on the news, talking
to the press, launching his campaign by telling the whole
damned world the deal I talked to him about today, before I
had a chance to run it by you. And what if you don't buy it?
Christ, what if I don't buy it?"

"He did, buddy, he did. Did it real good so that we don't
have no choice. If I don't go along, I look like a first-class
jerk, and he'll shove it up my ass, too, and have no problem
putting me away."

A thought flashed through Seymour's mind, an idea he
rejected but that insisted upon being voiced.

"Junior, you need to tell me one thing straight. Did you talk
to O'Riley before today?" He paused. "He told me he was the
one who prosecuted you on the jewelry store robbery."

"What are you sayin?"

"I don't know. It just seems to me you should be more
upset than you are."

Junior stood up and paced. When he stopped in front of
Seymour, his body seemed coiled, ready to spring, but his
eyes were calm.

"I think I understand your problem, man, but it is defi-
nitely your problem. The way I see it, you did your job. You
got me off. I don't really care how."

"You haven't answered my question."

Junior leaned over Seymour. "Don't push me, man, don't ever push me. You gotta know the answer to that is no way."

"Good. Because if I think for a second you and he worked this thing out together, I'm outta here. So, we can forget that. Let's just think about where we are. I can file a motion. Have the charges dropped on procedural grounds."

"That's good lawyer talk, counselor. But it's my ass on the line. And even if you win, I lose. I wouldn't be able to take a deep breath before they got me for something else. So let's just say it's done, baby, it's done. We'll just have to live with it. Whether you want it, or I want it, don't make no difference." Junior sat down next to Seymour on the couch, bit off the end of a cigar, and lit it. Beneath the cloud of smoke he exhaled, he looked content.

Lois came in from the kitchen, wiping her hands on an apron. She smiled at Junior and leaned over to brush her lips against Seymour's cheek.

"Hey," she said, "what's the problem?"

"My counselor here don't like being used."

"There are worse things," Lois said. "It all depends on who's doing what to whom. Anyway, I've got my man, and we all have a friend in a high place."

"And going higher on our backs," Seymour snapped.

"Right," Junior said. "But sometimes, like momma says, when you're getting screwed you gotta enjoy the ride."

Seymour found it difficult to accept Lois in the domestic role she assumed serving them dinner, complete with wine, candles, and an afterdinner brandy, but somehow he understood that she was capable of changing her colors for any occasion, of being anything she wanted to for a purpose.

Over dinner, they talked of trivial things, how Lois was looking forward to staying home with the baby, how the old neighborhood had changed, the whereabouts of friends.

Only when Lois asked about Sammy did energy gather about the table, and when Seymour explained that his brother was a successful real estate attorney in California, Lois flashed an enigmatic smile.

"Maybe I should have held onto a good thing when I had it," she said.

Junior sneered. "Couldn't have been that good. Or maybe I was just that much better."

"Don't blow yourself up too much. You'll explode. I didn't know what the hell I wanted in those days, and Sammy was nice, very nice, like all the Lipps."

"Yes, nice," Junior said quietly, "but nice isn't always enough, is it Lois?"

"Maybe not," she said, and then turned to Seymour, "but some times, like tonight, it might be just fine." She asked Junior: "Don't you think Seymour should look up Rosalie. She's not very far away at all." Her voice flowed a warm stream of false concern, with just a ripple of mocking good humor. She looked at Seymour. "Rosalie would be thrilled to get a phone call from her ex-lover, the distinguished lawyer, especially now that he's been on television."

"I wasn't on," Seymour objected, "and I don't intend to be."

"Small difference. And anyway, don't be so sure O'Riley didn't dig up a picture of you somewhere, maybe from the college yearbook or something. But you were mentioned, and Rosalie must have seen the news. She's the type to watch every night while she prepares her lonely dinner. Why not give her a call?"

"I don't want Rosalie dragged into this mess."

"Don't worry," Lois smiled. "Rosalie will be just fine. Take my word. Remember Rosalie and I go back a long way together, Rosalie and me and the whole Constantino family."

The slap startled Seymour. He had not seen Junior's arm come sweeping across the table until the open palm hit Lois' cheek. He grabbed Junior's wrist, but it was like holding the

arm of a marble statue. Junior stared at Lois, his eyes ablaze.
"I told you never to talk about that."

Lois shrugged, and Junior turned to Seymour who was still
holding his wrist. "Easy, hero, it's all over, and it's none of
your business."

They sat in silence for a few moments, and then Lois continued as though nothing had interrupted her conversation.

"Yes, Seymour, I think you should call Rosalie tomorrow,
first thing."

"Why not tonight, if you think it's such a fuckin' good
idea." He got up from the table and slammed his chair in.

Lois reached over to him and took his hand, soothingly.

"Tonight would be too soon," she said. "Don't take things
so hard. We're all friends, aren't we?"

"That's it, that's the way," Junior agreed. "Tonight,
you're our guest. Trust me. I'll choose what's right for you."

"No thanks," Seymour said. "I think, if anything, I will
have to choose for you."

Lois leaned over the table again closer to Seymour. "Call
Rosalie tomorrow. Tomorrow is soon enough for her."

After dinner, Junior took out a cube of hash and a small
onyx pipe. He reached into his pocket, pulled out a knife,
and flicked it open. With one swift motion, he sliced a chunk
of hash off the cube and ground it between his fingers. Then
he tamped it into the bowl of the pipe, and lit it. The smoke
curled up softly toward the ceiling, thick and pungent.

Seymour grabbed Junior's thick forearm. "I just got you
off a drug rap."

Junior looked down at Seymour's hand on his arm. "Now,
that's twice you've grabbed me, and that's twice too much,
for anyone, even you." Then he smiled again. "The rap,
man, was for dealin', not taking a blast with friends."

They sat before the television at eleven o'clock to watch

the news. Seymour did not remember leaving the kitchen to walk into the living room. He recalled that after Junior had inhaled the smoke, he had handed the pipe to him, and that he had taken a deep drag that had left his mouth and throat dry. He had coughed a bit and then inhaled again, enjoying the buzz.

At first the sensation was tamer than he remembered, but then he noticed that he was seeing things with great clarity. The scar on the bridge of Junior's nose leaped out at him and bared its jagged edge. The color seemed to redden on the scar and Junior's face began to glow. He looked at Lois and her breasts heaved in a slow and measured movement. He did not feel particularly aroused, more intrigued in an almost remote way by the protruding nipples that poked at the cotton of her top.

When O'Riley's features flashed onto the television screen, Seymour felt a sympathetic smile began to curl his own lips. O'Riley looked ridiculous with his tweed cap perched on one side of his head. His teeth appeared extraordinarily bright, at first, but the more Seymour looked, the more he noticed their unevenness. The incisors were long and yellowed like the fangs of an old wolf.

He was talking about Seymour and Junior, and then Lois and the baby. He said he could not provide pictures because he wanted to protect the "struggling family's" identity. Seymour heard his own name several times, but he lost the context even though O'Riley's words echoed as though they had been uttered into a marvelously acoustic tunnel. Seymour could not determine whether the words were coming from the far or near end of the tunnel because the sound varied in intensity, always clear, but ranging from an almost unbearable volume to a loud stage whisper, with always the suggestion of a laugh or a snarl, and then he realized that some of the laughter he heard was coming from the other side of the sofa.

Junior's smile had widened so that it split the lower
portion of his face from the upper. His jaw appeared elon-
gated, and his dark eyes burned deeply in the olive of his
face. Lois was sitting on the other side of Junior, and
Seymour had to lean forward to see her. She smiled at him
and opened her mouth to talk. Although he saw her red lips
and pink tongue moving slowly, he could not distinguish her
words. He settled back to look at the television and tried to
bring O'Riley back into focus, but he could only make out
the imposing line of microphones that filled the screen in
front of the prosecutor's face. When he next looked over to
Junior, he had disappeared. Lois was stretched out on the
couch, staring at him. Her fingers began at her lips and
trailed down over her breasts, pausing for a long moment,
and then reached the space between her legs. She rolled her
hips in the deep cushions of the sofa.

In the darkness of her bedroom, she undressed him and
sealed her flesh to his. He felt both oddly detached, as if he
were witnessing the sensations of another, and intensely
alive at each point of contact, as though for that moment
his whole being were concentrated wherever her lips or
fingers touched. They fell slowly onto the bed.

For some reason, Seymour was at first preoccupied with
the blanket, which had been neatly folded down. His skin
recoiled at the touch of the cool sheets. Then he heard the
low hum of the air conditioner and realized that he had been
sweating in the sultry air of the living room.

Lois turned him onto his back. Her hair shifted to one
side and brushed against his bare shoulder. It felt soft and
warm. She followed his eyes, and then dipped her head so
that her hair drifted over his chest pausing to tease each
nipple with just the tips of her hair.

The couch in her parents' apartment in Brooklyn flashed
into his consciousness, and he rolled away. Too many times,
in that place, he had allowed himself to be used, to be

humiliated—to be pleasured. He grabbed her by the shoulders and started to turn her on her back, but she resisted. They struggled for a moment, and then she laughed, softly against the hum of the air conditioner.

"I know," she whispered, "but not this time. This time it has to be our way, Junior's way."

He remembered her appearance in the lobby, the way her bare thighs had seemed to glow with a warmth he could feel, how her full-lipped smile had beckoned him, and he realized that he had given himself to her at that moment, whatever she might demand. Now it was clear that he would have to accept her as Junior's gift to him or not have her at all. He lay back and closed his eyes.

He felt her breath against his neck, and he pulled her down onto him, crushing her against his chest. She raised her upper body and he reached for her breasts. He found a nipple with each thumb and caressed it while thrusting his pelvis up. He squeezed one nipple a little harder and a thin bluish-white drop oozed onto his fingers. The pearl, just like your come, she had said, so sweet and white. He heard the springs creak and Lois' breath quicken, and then her warm flesh collapsed on him, feet locked for leverage, and then he felt only her hair blanketing his face.

Seymour awoke in the darkened room. He turned toward Lois, but the bed was empty. As he rolled back to his side, he felt a damp spot in the middle of the sheet. He ran his fingers over it and then alongside the inside of his thighs where his hairs were matted and stiff.

He tried to remember the warmth of the night, but it had left only a still damp stain on the sheet and an unclean feeling between his thighs. His body, which had felt such vital pleasure, now offended him with its leaden and stolid presence. He studied, as was his habit, the unusually smooth and white skin drawn over the end of his shortened foot.

The room in its air-conditioned seal, curtains drawn over the high basement windows, did not permit the outside to penetrate. He strained to hear signs of activity, trucks rumbling, birds chirping, kids shouting, anything, but all that reached his ears was the constant drone of the air conditioner. He forced himself to drop his feet over the side of the bed and onto the thinly carpeted floor. He looked down and saw that the carpet was the kind found in cheap motels, a skimpy, short shag that separated beneath his feet. He drew back the curtain and discovered that the sun was at a midmorning height, and that the street was alive with kids playing ball. He could see their mouths moving and their arms gesturing, but no sound reached through the window.

When he turned around, Junior was at the foot of the bed, his smile brilliant in the dim light.

"Hey, lover, rise and shine. You've been makin' love to momma and forgettin' me."

"Where's Lois?"

"She's gone, as she came."

"But where?"

"Don't sweat it, man. Like I said, she was here when I told her to be."

Seymour shuddered. "And gone the same way."

Junior beamed. "You got it babe, you got it."

Seymour found Lois in the kitchen, sitting at the table and wearing a plain terrycloth robe, open at the top so that she could nurse the baby. The baby had her right breast firmly between its hands, and its mouth was working rhythmically on the nipple. Lois was looking down at the tiny face and murmuring a string of nonsense words. She looked perfectly content.

He sat down next to her, and she smiled at him as though she had just met him on the street after not having seen him for a long time. The smile said that the night before had never happened, but the sight of the baby greedily working at her breast stirred his memory, and he felt again her milk between his fingers. She studied his face, and as though she had read his thoughts and insisted on deflecting them she turned her head toward the refrigerator.

"If you want some breakfast, you'll have to fix it yourself. Junior has already eaten, and I can't get up. But help yourself to whatever you want in the fridge."

"I think I'll just have a cup of coffee. And then I'd like to talk to you."

"Oh, that sounds serious, counselor. What should we discuss? The weather? The virtues of breast-feeding? You know that's overrated. In fact, it's a real pain in the ass." She shifted the baby to her other breast. "It's about time for Jenny to switch to bottles, don't you think?"

He struggled for a response, and then gave it up.

"Lois, I mean, how can you just sit there and talk to me about breast-feeding versus bottles?"

She offered a brilliantly cold smile.

"So, what the hell, what's the big deal? We got it on last night. Does that mean I should have a glow in my eyes this morning? What are you complaining about? You got paid, you passed Go and spent the night on Park Place. Don't be such an asshole!"

Seymour poured himself a cup of coffee and sat back down at the table.

"You're right. I guess it doesn't matter, after all. You were just my client's way of making my fee. Let's say," he looked for an amount that would hurt, "a fifty dollar retainer. It's not much, but probably all the poor bastard can afford."

She raised her hand from the baby for a second, and then brought it back behind her head before she let it relax to her side.

"Is that what the son-of-a-bitch said this morning, that he had sent me to you?"

Seymour nodded.

"Don't believe everything he says, you should know that by now. And don't underestimate either of us, especially me."

"Little danger of that."

He finished his coffee and sat across the table from her. She looked at him as though he were a female friend who had just dropped by for a morning visit, two housewives ready to talk about babies and grocery bills.

She shifted in her seat, and reached for a pack of cigarettes from the table. He fished in his pocket for a light, but she indicated she didn't need one. While still cradling the baby, now asleep, in one arm, she turned the pack over with her free hand and slid out a cigarette. Picking up a book of matches, she bent one stalk down, and lit it herself.

"You never know when you're gonna need a light and not have a man handy. You know what I mean?" she laughed.

He studied her face, waiting for another change in the shifting surface: the seductive temptress who aroused him, the street hard hustler whose brittle smile repelled all contact, the nursing mother absorbed in her baby, the old friend with only his best interests at heart. None of them were real, but like a wanderer in a carnival hall of mirrors, he continued to look for the source of the illusions.

"Let me ask you a question," he said. "One that goes back to the old days."

She frowned, but he needed to try to elicit an answer, or failing that, a response that would bring her out.

"Do you remember telling me about a ring?"

She narrowed her eyes as though concentrating, but then she shook her head.

"A pearl ring?" he prodded. "One that you had seen in a jewelry store window?"

"I don't think so." She smiled brightly. "Were we going to get engaged? With a pearl ring?"

"You were intrigued by its color."

Recognition flashed in her eyes.

"Oh, that. Funny how I remember telling you I wanted it. But I said a lot of things in those days. For a certain effect. What of it?"

"Only this." He recognized that she would not offer him the response he wanted, but if he couldn't pierce her surface, perhaps he could peel it back a little. "Whatever effect you intended, I took your request, pardon the phrase, to heart."

"You always were the romantic." Her lips curved between a smile and a sneer.

"Right. But here's the point. I mentioned it to Junior."

She beamed.

"Of course. You two were such buddies, kind of blood kin, your blood anyway." She paused. "Now let me guess. He said that if you had the balls you'd get it for me, steal it if you had to. Right?"

Seymour nodded. Maybe she knew after all.

"I'm guessing, of course," she said. "Junior has always been shy about talking about you and him. But I do know him. And you."

"Meaning?"

"Let me, see. He laid a macho trip on you and you rose to the bait."

He permitted himself a half smile, sensing that he almost had her trapped—the arrogant mouse nosing at the cheese, confident that it will beat the steel trigger.

"Yes," he said. "And what else do you guess?"

She furrowed her brows, and looked at him through half opened eyes.

"I don't know. That's as far as I can go. I don't remember getting the ring. So your better sense must have won out."

He shook his head.

"No. My better sense was out to lunch. *We* went after the ring."

Her face darkened.

"You mean *that* time."

He nodded.

"Jesus," she said, her voice soft in disbelief, "I never took you for such a fool. Or him. I always thought he just hit some bad luck. But this does make more sense. That you were involved."

"Right," he said. "Now you're beginning to get it. It was almost like he knew we'd get caught, like he wanted us to."

She jumped.

"So he could save your ass. Even the score. For the cherry bomb."

"Exactly. And here I sit."

She recovered and turned sultry.

"And is that all?"

He considered leaving it like that, for payback, but he relented.

"No, not only that. Of course, for you too."

She tried to hide her relief behind a hard smile.

"More that than the other, if I'm any judge." She nudged his foot under the table. "Junior blew it away, and I made love to it. What could be simpler than that?"

"Nothing at all," he said. The door opened, and Lois turned to Junior.

"Our counselor, here, was just saying that all he had to do was get you a job, and that'll be that."

He followed her eyes to the doorway where Junior had appeared. He was carrying a bag of groceries from which he pulled out a six-pack of Micheloeb.

"Better than my usual brew, but I thought I should get something special. In honor of the occasion."

"What occasion?" Seymour asked.

"Well, fuckit, it's not every day a boy gets a new daddy." He turned to Lois, "Right, momma?"

Lois forced a laugh. "Sure, Junior, whatever you say."

Junior twisted the cap off a bottle and handed it to Seymour. The bottle was cold, and vapor rose from the open neck. He threw down a mouthful, and it felt good.

"That's right, drink up, my man. We all got to take good care of each other now."

Seymour finished the beer and got up. The room was warm, and a dizzying blend of traffic noise and children shouting came in from the street through the open door. He felt the blood drain from his face for a moment.

"Well," he said slowly, "Daddy's got to go to work. He's got to see what he can do to get junior a job."

Junior's laugh spilled out in a spray of beer. He wiped his mouth with the back of his hand.

"Don't make it anything too tough," he said, "because I've been out of the job market for a very long time."

Seymour smiled and turned to the door, but Lois caught up with him before he could leave.

"Thanks for everything," she said loudly, and then she brushed his ear with her lips. "I just want you to know that I really am grateful. Not for him, for me," she whispered.

The house was surprisingly unpretentious, the smallest on a block that backed the ocean beach. When Seymour had found a listing for Schotelheim in the phone directory giving a street address in this private community, he had imagined the old lawyer's house to be grand, something in keeping with his estimation of the man. But the house he now approached through a tangle of weeds and marshy grass that had overgrown the front walk was little more than a summer cottage. A mosquito buzzed around his head, and he swiped at it. To his surprise, he felt his palm graze the insect, and the buzzing stopped. He stood quietly for a moment, but he heard nothing.

"Very good," a deep voice offered from the doorway. "But I'm afraid if we sit out back to enjoy the breeze off the water, you'll have more of that kind of work than you bargained for."

They settled for the back room of the house, and sat across from each other in worn but comfortable easy chairs that flanked a fireplace. The other walls in the room were lined with shelves that sagged beneath hundreds of musty looking books, and that part, at least, coincided with Seymour's imaginings. The surf roared in at them through the windows on either side of the fireplace, and when it receded it was replaced by the pinging of insects against the screens.

"I like this room best in the winter," Schotelheim said, "because then I can get a good fire crackling, while above it I can still hear the ocean." He glanced toward the window. "When Marta was alive, we'd walk that beach just about every morning, all year round, and the winter was always the best." His eyes drifted for a moment, and then focused on Seymour.

"Well, my boy, you haven't sought me out here to listen to me reminisce about my wife or to share impressions of nature. And I have to be careful, you know. Like all old people living alone I tend to make every guest compensate for all those who haven't visited by listening to a monologue that is not of the slightest interest to him. You had better keep me on the track." He laughed, his bass voice filling the room. "How are you getting on?"

Seymour took a deep breath. "I've decided to strike out on my own."

He waited as Schotelheim processed the news, recognizing that the old man saw the iceberg beneath the tip he had revealed.

"In fact, I already have my first client. You might say he was kind of imposed on me. I think you'll understand after I tell you the circumstances."

A moth had made its way into the room and banged

against the inside of a lamp shade, fluttering from side to side but unable to find the way out.

"I feel something like that moth," Seymour said. "Trapped, and about to be fried on the bulb. I know that this arrangement with Junior was not established correctly. But I also sense that my hands are tied, that O'Riley has me in a box."

"Not only the prosecutor, if I have understood you correctly. In fact, he is the least of the your problems." Schotelheim had listened silently to Seymour's story, and encouraged by his concern, Seymour had told him more than he had intended, more than just the immediate problem, something of his past relationship with Junior as well. He had almost said more, but stopped short of recreating the scenes of the past night.

"You know," Schotelheim said, "that there is nothing I can suggest that will help you. You already have stated the legal situation, quite accurately. You have asked me whether you should undertake an arrangement that places you in a rather bizarre guardianship role." He paused, and then spoke very distinctly. "Your legal exposure is nil. There is no way you can be held responsible for Junior's actions, even were he to assassinate the Pope while you were walking together down Fifth Avenue past St. Patrick's. Your moral exposure, on the other hand, is very grave indeed. But that is a matter for you to decide. As you knew, before you came here."

"I guess I did, but I needed to hear somebody else say it."

"Yes, and now I have. I can only wish you wisdom in your choice. And, such as it is, my help if you should feel you need it again."

Before he said good-bye, Seymour walked onto the beach with the old man. They stood for a few minutes, just listening to the roar of the ocean.

"I don't know if it will help," Schotelheim said, "but I can tell you that once I was in a box as you describe."

"And?"

The old man shrugged, as though a weight from a long time ago still pressed down on him.

"I did what I had to do, as you have." He turned toward the shore.

Seymour gave voice to a thought that had been forming during the whole conversation.

"You might not understand this, sir, and I mean it as a compliment, but I feel as though I've been speaking to a figure in an old print I have hanging on my wall."

Schotelheim raised his eyebrows.

"It's a print of ancient rabbis, arguing the Talmud," Seymour added.

The old man seized Seymour's shoulders and squeezed with unexpected strength.

"Would that I had their wisdom," he said softly. "I would die a happy man."

$\triangledown$

Three

T HE RING OF THE phone broke into Seymour's thoughts
and he waited impatiently for Dorothy to pick it up. With a
start, he realized that he was sitting behind the huge, scarred
oak desk he had just bought for his new office in a converted
warehouse on Smith Street, just a short walk from the court
building on Schermerhorn, and that if he didn't pick up the
phone, nobody would.

O'Riley's voice snaked through the receiver.

"How's our boy doing?" he asked.

"Our boy is just fine. He's working here in this building.
As a custodian."

"What!" O'Riley's voice rose. "Perfect. Couldn't be better.
I was afraid you'd get him something too cushy."

Seymour picked up a newly sharpened pencil, held it
between his fingers, and snapped it in half.

"Look," he said. "It was my understanding that you're
out of our lives now. You've got what you wanted. You're
ahead in the polls."

"Never far enough." O'Riley chuckled. "Anyway, I'd like
to ask you a favor." He paused, but Seymour did not reply.
"After all, we are on the same side of the law, aren't we? I
would like, since we are dependent on electronic media, to

send over my media crew, at your convenience, of course, for a follow-up. You know, our chap pushing a broom, looking earnestly into the camera, earning an honest dollar, and as happy as he can be to be able to make a living by the sweat of his brow."

Seymour rolled the two pieces of the pencil across his desk top and lined them up so that the break was scarcely visible.

"Don't even think about it," he said slowly. "If they show up, I'll make sure they hear and see things that will cause this whole affair to blow up in your face. Maybe Lois in her hooker's clothes with a screaming and dirty baby on her hip. You'll have to manage without us."

Seymour imagined the prosecutor's expression, perhaps just a pull on his ascot before he continued.

"You may be making a mistake, a very big mistake, my lad," he said. "Somebody in my position can be of great assistance to you or, more to the point, an even greater hindrance."

"Thanks for the advice, but I guess I'll have to take my chances."

"Just think about it. You know where to reach me." O'Riley's voice disappeared in the click of the receiver.

It was less than a month since his conversation with O'Riley in the restaurant on Mott Street. In that time, he had accepted guardianship of Junior, resigned his job, borrowed five thousand dollars from his brother, Sammy, as start-up money for his own practice, and found this office, and along with it, a job for Junior, who now filled the doorway, leaning over his broom, a pile of dust and scraps of paper at his feet.

"I thought you would have been gone by now," Seymour said.

"Overtime," Junior smiled. "You know these honest wages don't stretch too far."

"Yes, but they'll keep us both out of trouble."

"Right you are," Junior smiled. "But say, you don't mind if I skip your office this time, seeing how you're still working, and besides there hasn't been much traffic in here."

He didn't wait for an answer, but instead pushed his broom up the hall. He stopped every few steps to make sure that he was leaving the floor clean behind him. He was doing this all for Seymour's benefit, as though they shared a private and ridiculous joke.

A few moments after Junior disappeared, an attractive woman, tall and elegant, knocked on the open door. She was wearing a white linen dress that set off her deeply tanned skin, and a bright blue scarf that picked up the color of her eyes.

"Excuse me," she said. "I'm looking for a Mr. Seymour Lipp."

"You've found him," Seymour said. He noticed that the scarf was held in place by a diamond ring through which the ends had been drawn.

"Thank goodness," she sighed. "I've been looking all through this building. I passed by this office before, but there was no name on the door, and it was closed, so I went upstairs, downstairs, everywhere. I was just about to give up when I met that," she paused, "custodian, I guess, although he doesn't look like one."

She spoke with the ease of a prep school education, just a hint of a lisp, but each word distinct.

"Nor work much like one," Seymour said.

She seemed to consider for a moment.

"A man like that," she said, "should have no trouble finding more suitable employment."

"Maybe so," Seymour replied quickly, as he pictured Junior stuffed into a chauffeur's uniform holding a limousine door open for this young woman, "but he's going to have to stay where he is for a while."

The woman's face registered a question and Seymour covered the awkward pause.

"Well, why don't you come in, and tell me what I can do for you."

"Oh, I don't think that will be necessary."

Seymour started to object, fearing that he had insulted his first walk-in client, but she smiled.

"I mean, all I want is the key to the warehouse space upstairs. The landlord said you had it."

"Of course," Seymour said. He took the key out of the top drawer of his desk. "He left it with me for Mrs. Levine. That must be you."

"Mrs. Levine," she corrected, "with a long *i*, like in wine, we like to say."

"As you wish," Seymour said. "Do you know the way?"

"Oh, I think so. I really hope this space is adequate. She looked at the exposed pipes overhead. "Do you think there will be pipes upstairs, as well?"

"I'm afraid so," Seymour said. "This is an old building, some kind of factory at some point, I suppose, and that's how they used to make them. Pipes everywhere."

"Well, we'll have to do something about that. Maybe we can drop the ceiling, hide them somehow. My husband's furs and those awful pipes. It just won't do."

"Thanks for the key," she said. "I'm sure I'll see you again. Soon." She started down the hall, but in a moment Junior was at her side.

"Allow me, Mrs. Levine," he said, drawing out the second syllable. "I'll take you up the freight elevator."

Seymour watched them enter the elevator and saw Junior's hand brush against her hip as the door closed. He shook his head, wondering if O'Riley knew what he had bought into with Junior.

Seymour had worked late one night, and the streets outside his building were blanketed in a thick fog. He headed toward his subway stop, enjoying the clatter of his shoes on the cobblestones. He was halfway down a street little wider than an alley when he stopped to light a cigarette.

"Hey, man, you got a light?"

Seymour looked around him, but he was already encircled, two in front, two behind, teenagers and all smaller than he, but too many. He held out his lighter toward the ringleader whose features were hidden by the fog. He flicked the lighter and the flame danced off a gold tooth.

"Thanks, man," the cool voice said.

"No problem," Seymour said, and he took a step straight ahead. The ringleader and another youth cut him off.

"Hey, man what's your hurry?" the gold tooth asked.

Seymour didn't answer. He threw his shoulder into the one next to the ringleader and butted him back. He started to run, but after a few steps he tripped and a hand grabbed his coat and started to spin him around. He permitted himself to be turned, and at the same time threw his fist at the first head he saw. He felt it crash solidly against bone and flesh, and a shape crumbled to the ground. Then the others were on him, and he was wrestled against a wall. Something hard glanced off the side of his head and he slumped to the ground.

"Now, man, why did you have to go and do that?"

Seymour looked up at the ringleader.

"What were you going to ask me for next? The time?"

"No, asshole, your watch. What you think?" Seymour followed the voice to a figure behind the ringleader.

"Hey, no," the gold tooth said soothingly, "don't pay him no attention. We don't want much from you. Just a few dollars, whatever you have."

Seymour reached into his jacket pocket for his wallet, but a hand closed over his arm.

"Don't trouble yourself, man. I'll get it."

The ringleader took the wallet, lifted the cash and credit cards efficiently, handed them to the one Seymour had hit, and tossed the wallet into the street.

"There's not much here." He sighed. "The plastic is a lot of trouble for our immediate needs. And this," he held the thin wad of bills between his finger, "now has to pay for some cosmetic surgery for my man over there. You made him even uglier. You shouldn't have done that."

Seymour had started to get up. He didn't see the kick aimed at his belly until it was too late, and he collapsed with pain shooting across his ribs. He gasped for breath. A fist smashed into his face, and he felt his eye begin to close. In a blind fury, he hurled himself at the figure in front of him and they rolled over on the pavement until he forced himself on top. He clubbed at the flash of gold and felt blood flow over his torn knuckles. He raised his arm again. This time, though, several hands pulled him up and shoved him onto the ground. Another kick landed in his ribs and he rolled over, covering his head.

He heard a couple of thuds, but felt nothing. Then, for a moment there was silence, followed by the scrape of shoes running down the street. He looked up and saw a thick arm locked around gold tooth's neck, cradling the head, while another hand flashed a long and lean blade up to the face.

"What do you say, my man? Should I cut him?"

Seymour squinted at Junior and tried to speak. But Junior didn't wait. With one quick motion, he brought the blade across the ringleader's cheek in a six-inch arc from his ear to the corner of his mouth.

"Maybe, now, your girlfriend won't find you so pretty," Junior said in a voice half snarl and half laugh. "I marked you so I'll remember you. If I ever see your ugly face again, I'll cut you worse, so you'll have nothing for your girlfriend." He stood up and smashed his heavy laborer's shoe into the ringleader's groin. "You understand what I mean, man?" Seymour staggered to his feet and stumbled over to Junior. Junior turned to him and steadied him.

"Easy, my man, it's all over," he said.

Seymour looked down at gold tooth. Blood ran from the slice. He lay on his side, his hands between his legs, and his mouth half open. There was a gap where his gold tooth had been. Seymour looked down at his own hand and saw that he had a ragged cut on his index finger, just below the knuckle.

"You popped him good." Junior smiled. He leaned over, picked up Seymour's wallet, and unfolded it. He shrugged and tossed it to Seymour.

"Picked the green clean, man, but at least like they say, you still have your health."

Seymour passed his hand over his bruised face.

"At least what's left of it." He glanced at his assailant who lay still on the ground, his eyes closed.

"I don't think we have to worry about him no more," Junior said. "He's stupid, but I don't think he's that dumb. Anyway, let's get the hell out of here."

"Do you think we should just leave him here, like this?" Seymour asked.

"What do you want to do, call an ambulance, and then have to answer a bunch of questions. Before you know it, they'll be saying we started the whole thing. There's two of us and one of him."

Seymour began to say something about how ridiculous that version of the incident would be, but then he remembered O'Riley's unctuous voice and he stuffed his empty wallet into his pocket without looking at the inert figure on the street.

Seymour sat at his desk, his hand bandaged and his whole body stiff with pain. He had reviewed the file on the land-lord/tenant case he would argue on behalf of the tenant until he had to conclude for the hundredth time that the landlord, a Mr. Goode, held all the legal cards. As he pushed the file to a corner of his desk, he heard a gentle knock on the door, and looked up.

"I hope you don't mind my stopping by. Junior called the other day and told me where I could find you. He mentioned something about a fight, and, well, here I am. I don't know exactly why."

Seymour noticed her eyes first, even deeper and more lustrous than he had remembered. Beneath her beret, her hair was cut stylishly short, revealing delicate gold hoop earrings. She was wearing a tan blazer and a plaid skirt.

"Looks something like the old school outfit, doesn't it?" She smiled. "We librarians are supposed to dress discreetly, you know."

"Maybe," he said, coming forward to embrace her. "But you'll always be special, Rosalie, particularly when you are wearing this." He ran his fingers over the beret, and then stroked her hair.

"I didn't know if you would remember. Anyway, I had to look all over for it before I found it stuffed on the top shelf of my closet."

The thought that he, too, might be only a memory retrieved from a dusty storage place stung.

"Of course, I remember it," he said. "You were wearing it the last time I saw you." He paused. "I remember that, and your father's rather large fist aimed at my head."

She smiled sadly, and her voice was gentle.

"That was a difficult time, for both of us. I'd like to talk with you, if you have time. Maybe we could get some lunch."

Seymour walked back to his desk, and picked up his appointment calendar. He studied it for a moment, and then held it up to her so that she could see the page, filled only with doodlings.

"Well," he said, "I think I might be able to squeeze in a day or two before my next client comes wandering by."

"That bad," she said.

"That new, anyway." He put the book down, and picked up a little wooden box. "You know what's in here?"

"The key to your swiss bank account?"

He smiled and opened the box for her.

"It's not mine," he said, taking the gold tooth out of the box. "It used to belong to a particularly stubborn young man, who had his mind set on mugging me until your brother happened by, and together we managed to disabuse him of the notion."

Rosalie shuddered.

"I know," he said, "And I did try to run, which was a better thought, but I didn't get too far. I tripped and these guys were on me, and then Junior came along."

Seymour opened his desk drawer and pulled out a brown bag.

"It's a little early for my table to be ready at Twenty-One. Would you mind the Promenade? I frequent a certain bench."

Rosalie opened her pocketbook and showed the corner of her lunchbag.

"Just what I had in mind," she said.

Seymour pulled the crust off his bread and tossed it to the pigeons strolling in front of their bench. There was a brief flurry of wings and angry cooing, and then one bird emerged with piece of bread and strutted on. The others eyed Seymour expectantly for a moment, and then waddled off.

"I've thought about our last night together, a lot," he said. He expected a recrimination, at least in her eyes, something to ask why he had never called, not once, in all this time. But her face betrayed no anger.

"I have, too. But it just wasn't right, then. And it wasn't only our families' opposition."

"Well, for a while, we were Brooklyn's version of Romeo and Juliet. But you're right. That wasn't the cause."

"I think we both knew that. And then you went your way, and I, after a while, got married."

Seymour started.

"Is that so miraculous?" she asked, her voice mockingly angry.

"Of course not," he recovered. "It's just that I think of you only from that time. As if you and I have just said good-bye, and you are walking away, your beret perched on your head, and me sitting like a fool in that Packard."

She leaned toward him.

"How can you blame yourself? And I wasn't ready for anything. Except that I knew I had to get out of that house. And so, I guess, I married Timothy Michael O'Grady. My parents had a little trouble swallowing the name. But at least, you know, he wasn't Black. Or even a Protestant."

"Or, thank God, Jewish," Seymour smiled.

"No," she said seriously, "maybe that would have been tougher for them to accept. But then when I got divorced, my mother couldn't understand it, of course, and my father, well, he'd probably have tried to beat me if he could have stood up straight long enough. They moved out to the Island a few years ago. At the time Junior was looking for a place to live, but you know all about that. We don't talk much, really not at all. I send cards for birthdays, and holidays, but I don't call." She paused. "I think," she said slowly, "that they've buried me."

"As for Timothy Michael, well, it wasn't that hostile, nothing like that. He was a good kid, and I was a kid. You know, one of those kinds of things."

"It's never that easy," he said softly, the sentence falling hard between them.

"Oh, I see," she said, "that bad. For you."

"It was."

"And is?"

"Sometimes," he conceded.

She took a can of juice out of her lunchbag and offered it to him.

"Are you okay?" she asked after a moment. "I mean," she glanced at his bruised face and bandaged hand, "about that."

He nodded, happy for the distraction. "Oh, sure. Nothing

serious." He finished the juice and squeezed the can flat beneath his shoe. "The thing is, here I am trying to get my own practice started, and I can't tell the police when I'm mugged. Your brother," he said quietly, "is a dangerous man."

"And you are involved with him. Again, after all these years. I saw that prosecutor on television, and I wanted to throw something at him." Her eyes flashed and her voice trembled. "Can't you get out of this mess somehow?"

"In time. Right after the election, when O'Riley will be off our backs. Anyway, Junior did help me out. He might have saved my life."

She took the bandaged hand gently to her lips, and then brought her face close to his.

"That's the way he is, at least there is that part of him that is loyal to his friends." She forced a smile. "Sometimes more than they want."

He nodded, anxious for her to continue. He had stopped thinking about them as sister and brother. In his mind, he had separated her from her family.

"I know my brother, please be careful." She took his face between her hands. "He's reckless. He loves to play dangerous games." She started to look down, a faint blush on her cheeks. "But, of course, you know that. Anyway, I wanted to tell you that I do appreciate your helping him. But not if it's going to hurt you."

"I understand," he said.

"Promise me something, please."

"Anything."

"Get in touch with me right away if anything else goes wrong. Believe it or not, Junior sometimes listens to me."

"I will," he said. "Right now I'm trying to keep him away from a rich, spoiled, and bored young woman."

"Anybody you might be interested in?"

"Only," he said, "from a distance. Besides she's married."

Her face darkened. "And Junior's after her?"

"I think so."

"That would be just like him. He's never happy with what he's got, or what other people have. It's the challenge, I think. He wants to see what he can get away with."

Seymour felt the anger and resentment begin to build in him, but he forced a quietness in his voice.

"Look," he said. "I feel like this is an old story. I just hope he doesn't fuck up too badly until I can be free of him, once and for all. But I want you to know that I don't want to be free of you. Do you think we can try again?" He drew her to him and kissed her.

"I was hoping you might say something like that. If you hadn't, I would have said it for you."

"Excuse me, Rosalie," Seymour said. "I can't hear you well. There's some kind of construction going on on the floor above. Anyway, I'll see you tonight."

He hung up the phone and walked out into the hallway. All week, workers—carpenters, electricians, plumbers—had been trooping by on their way to the new showroom for Phil's Fur Palace, soon to be open to the public right above his head. And every day, as he tried to work, he was assaulted by the whine of power tools and the crash of the old plaster walls as they were pulled down.

On the stairs, he stopped a workman who was so covered with plaster dust only his eyes were visible in his face. From the stoop in his back, Seymour could see that he was not young.

"When will the work be done?" he asked.

The workman shrugged. "Three, four weeks, a year, who knows? You should see what she's doing to the place. You wouldn't recognize it."

"That's just where I was going," Seymour replied.

The worker brushed some dust from his cheek.

"Messy stuff, this old plaster," he said, "but when it's right there's nothing like one of those old walls, smooth and solid. Elegant, you know? I used to be a plasterer, but now there's no work. Everyone's using this new hollow shit. Hear the guy in the next apartment fart. But that's what they want. So I tear it down and put the cardboard up."

At the top of the stairs, Seymour encountered a cloud of dust through which other workmen moved, some walking, and other swinging their arms in purposeful motions directing invisible tools. The whole floor had been gutted. Seymour looked up, and saw that a new ceiling was being installed to hide the thick pipes. He picked his way through the rubble on the floor and found Mrs. Levine.

"Oh, Mr. Lipp. What do you think?"

He considered. "Well, I can't say that I can see very much right now." He brushed a flake of plaster from his sleeve."

She began to laugh but it degenerated into a giggle. "I know it's a mess, but it'll be worth it." She stepped closer to him and brushed some dust from his hair. Her hand was soft and he could smell a delicate perfume in the hollow of her wrist. Her fingers trailed behind his ear for a moment, before she moved away. He noticed that her eyes were bright but unfocused, and that she had to fight to control another giggle.

"I hope Phil likes it when he sees how far they've gotten," she managed to say. "Of course, he drew up all these plans. He knew exactly what he wanted. But then he got so busy at the main store on 34th Street, and there was that burglary in the Astoria store. He's just had to leave everything in my hands."

The words tumbled out without thought, but she now seemed in control again, and he decided to be charitable and ascribe her odd behavior to nervousness. He could still feel the touch of her fingers on his neck.

"You look like you're enjoying the experience," he said.

"Can I tell you something?" she asked, coming closer again.

Seymour felt as though she were drawing him into her troubled orbit, but he nodded. "Phil usually tries to keep me out of his business. But I like being involved. Especially here. The help is so nice. That one custodian, Junior, he's always coming around, asking if he can do anything."

Seymour chose his words carefully. He did not want to alarm her, but something in her voice urged him to speak.

"I'd be careful of him if I were you."

She broke into a fit of laughter.

"But you're old friends, aren't you? He said you were."

"Something like that."

"Well, then, you should know that he wouldn't hurt a fly. No one with eyes like his could be dangerous."

"Maybe not. But I am being serious."

He took in the elegant curve of her lips in her tight jeans, and the way her shirt was unbuttoned to reveal a glimpse of her breasts.

"I usually know what I'm doing, Mr. Lipp."

"I guess you do," he said. "I hope so."

"I will be careful," she said over her shoulder, as she turned to walk away.

The work on the showroom continued, and after a while, Phil started coming by to check its progress, first every two or three days and then daily as the opening of his new outlet approached. He was, in Seymour's eyes, overstuffed, overly pleased with himself, and arrogant, although his manners were perfectly friendly. Emily introduced him to Seymour as "Mr. Levine," and Phil smiled in satisfaction, as though he expected Seymour to recognize him as *the* Phil Levine, king of the discount fur business. He dressed in expertly tailored suits that could not quite conceal his substantial paunch, and when he offered his hand to Seymour it was warm but soft. It was clear to Seymour that Phil viewed his wife as an elegant accessory. Emily treated him with a superficial warmth beneath which Seymour detected a tinge of contempt.

For some reason, Seymour asked if they had children. He expected them to say yes, but he or she was at boarding school in Boston. But they looked at each other for a moment, and the space between them seemed charged with antipathy. Phil recovered first.

"No," he laughed. "Maybe some time soon. I guess we've been too busy to think of that."

Emily smiled tensely. "Yes, too busy. Phil is so concerned about his business, you know. And I'm in no hurry. Children are such a responsibility. Of course, Daddy would so like to have a grandson to leave all his things to."

It seemed to him, at that moment at least, that Emily had no intention of burdening herself with any more of oleaginous Phil than she already had.

Junior had largely receded into his responsibilities. He would stop by to see Seymour occasionally, but as the election approached, with O'Riley the clear favorite, they both recognized that this arrangement would soon terminate. Seymour had expected Junior to chafe under the bondage of his job, but instead he appeared to be happy.

One day in late October, a couple of weeks before the election, Seymour looked up from the pile of papers he was reviewing on his desk to find Junior silent and still, leaning on his broom, in the doorway to his office.

"You might knock, or something," Seymour said.

"I was about to, counselor, but I didn't want to disturb you right away. How's business? Picking up?"

Seymour looked down at his papers.

"Some. I'm working on a case that might interest you. It involves a landlord who wants to evict a tenant for nonpayment of rent, but the tenant claims that certain repairs to his sink have to be made under the lease."

"Don't sound too interesting to me," Junior said. "Why the fuck should I care about somebody's sink?"

"No reason. Only," Seymour paused. "the landlord's name is Goode."

Junior did not respond.

"Well," Seymour continued, "I guess you are not so intimate with Mrs. Levine as to know her maiden name."

Junior's face broke into a grin.

"Not a likely subject of conversation," he said. "But I know where you are in the case. You're on the side of the sucker with the sink, right?"

Seymour smiled. "Of course. Isn't that how I wound up with you?"

Junior leaned his broom against the door jamb and walked over to Seymour's desk. His dark eyes brooded for a moment.

"Anyway," he said, "what's going on between you and my sister?"

"Are you playing big brother, now?"

His intensity surprised Seymour.

"I don't play when it comes to family." But the serious mood disappeared as suddenly as it had come. "Naw," he smiled, "she don't need my help. But, I'm like, interested in love stories." His smile broadened into a smirk. "You and her gettin' it on?" he insisted.

Seymour stood up behind his desk and leaned forward as though to force Junior back.

"We've had lunch a few times, maybe a couple of movies, nothing heavy."

"That's too bad. She's a great girl. And you, I mean, you're my best friend."

The words flashed at Seymour as though they had danced off the sharp edge of Junior's knife.

"How's Lois and the baby doing?" he asked.

Junior frowned. "Great, just great, I guess. But you know

that baby has changed things. Lois, she's so concerned about that kid that sometimes she seems to forget she's got me to take care of. You know when that happens a man starts to look around. I mean if I was looking there's plenty, even right here in this building." He smirked again. "I seen the way you checked out Emily. Now there's a woman can make a man think things."

"She's out of your league," Seymour retorted. "High-class goods."

Junior laughed from deep in his belly.

"They don't teach you much in them schools do they. A fox like her always wants somebody like me, you know. Let me tell you she wouldn't be the first Park Avenue bitch I've had."

Seymour watched Junior's body as he spoke, and he could see the energy in muscularity, the invitation of the smile, and the mocking confidence in the eyes, and yes, maybe Emily, too, could have fallen under Junior's sway. Rather than anger, however, Seymour felt amusement. Soon none of this would be his concern or his problem.

"Just cool it until after the election when I can petition the court for your release from my guardianship. Okay?"

"Sure," Junior smiled. "But some things, especially good ones, just can't wait."

"Try to see that this one does. And watch out for her husband. He looks like a jerk, but he has money, and anyone with money is dangerous. That's my bit of wisdom for the day."

"Couldn't have said it better myself," Junior smiled, "but remember this, there are some things I can give a woman like Emily she can't get no place else." He retrieved his broom and headed down the hallway.

"Tough day in court?"

Emily Levine smiled at Seymour as they met in the

entrance to his building. As usual she was dressed elegantly, and provocatively, in a red and white flowered blouse that opened between her breasts, a matching scarf around her neck, and a flowing skirt slit above the knees in front. Although the day was gray, she was wearing dark sunglasses.

"Score another one for the bad guys. It's frustrating—" Seymour caught himself."

"You were about to say?" she encouraged.

"I could say a lot about what goes on." He smiled. "But in this case, the guy wearing the black hat was your father."

Her face darkened for a moment, but then she offered a practiced smile, such as she might wear in dealing with any of life's unpleasantries.

"Daddy has a lot of interests. Buildings he owns, and so many other things. I'm sure if you had had a chance to talk with him, you would have found him more than reasonable."

Her tone bordered on condescension, but Seymour detected as well an insincerity. He held her eyes until she turned away.

"I'm sure your father is a reasonable man, at least according to his lights. It may be a different story, viewed from my client's perspective."

"What I just said," she conceded, "is what we in the family always say. My father is very concerned with the family presenting a united front to the world. And since he pays the bills, all of them and quite generously, I usually toe the line."

"But?" he asked.

"Not always, and not with people I like. I am not always so reasonable as Daddy would like. And there are certain things Daddy doesn't understand, so he just won't pay."

He made the connection, but he wanted to be sure.

"And then what do you do?"

"I have my ways. I mean what's a girl to do when the merchant doesn't take plastic."

"Is your life, then, so tough? I wouldn't have thought so."

"Tough has nothing to do with it." She adjusted her scarf and Seymour thought he saw a red welt or scratch on her neck, but then she smoothed the fabric over her skin.

"Sometimes," he said, "Daddy might be right."

She measured him.

"You mean generally? Or that I should watch my step with your buddy."

"Both."

She laughed and then brought her face closer to his.

"Jealous."

"Sure, if that'll make you think about what you're doing."

She raised her hand again to the scarf as if to make sure it still covered her neck.

"Well, like they say, no pain, no gain."

"Meaning?"

She brought her finger to her chin as though pondering a question she had never before considered.

"Well, I guess it's like opposites explain each other, you know, something like my father holding on to what he has now because of where he started."

"But you?"

"Yes, that is a problem. I have to create my own opposites."

"I can understand that, to a point," he said slowly.

She was ahead of him.

"But, you want to say, maybe Junior is too much."

"That, and certainly the other."

Her face hardened.

"As for your friend, I can handle him, and my other friend is the one I can always count on. Anyway, why are you so damned interested?"

He had heard enough, for the moment.

"Junior likes to say that I'm always on the side of the underdog."

She threw back her head and laughed.

"And that's what you see in me?"

"Maybe so."

A gust of wind lifted her skirt for a moment, revealing her trim thighs. She waited a moment before patting it down, and then she ran her palms over her belly. When she saw his eyes follow her hands, she stopped in midmotion and turned to leave. Her whole body was lean and fit, except her rounded stomach.

"I've been so busy," she said over her shoulder, "that I just haven't had time to get to the gym like I usually do." She took a step away, and then turned back to him once more, lowering her glasses so she could focus on him better. "Thanks for the discretion," she said. "And people think chivalry is dead."

The next day Seymour arrived at his office early and found Junior in the basement in front of the custodian's closet. He was sitting on an overturned bucket, a cigarette in one hand, a beer can in the other.

"I think it's time we talked about your future," Seymour said. "Have you thought about getting another job?"

"Yeah," Junior answered, "they're gonna look at my record, and then show me the door." He smiled. "Maybe, I should just hold onto a good thing while I got it."

Seymour frowned. "I'm not sure that's such a terrific idea. We both know that you hate pushing a broom."

"I don't push it all that much."

"I've noticed."

"Anyway. There's the fringe benefits to consider."

"If you're talking about Emily," Seymour replied, "that's not going to last forever."

"No, it won't" Junior said slowly, and Seymour saw that his usually mocking eyes were dark. He considered for a moment and then took the plunge.

"You're dealing her drugs, aren't you?"

"Bitch tell you that?" Junior leaped to his feet and grabbed his broom as though it were a club.

"No, not exactly," Seymour said, "but she's obviously doing something."

Junior seemed to relax, though he still squeezed the handle of his broom.

"You got that one right, but then it don't take no rocket scientist to figure that."

"If you are her dealer, just cut it, that's all."

"Hey, man, have you ever seen her straight? It's not a pretty sight, I mean the fox can turn positively ugly."

"I haven't had the pleasure," Seymour snapped. "In any sense."

"No, you haven't, my man, and that's the word, pleasure." He leaned his weight on his broom as though it were a fence over which he intended to share a piece of gossip.

"And one thing more." He shook his head as though in disbelief. "The lady likes to play rough. You know what I mean?"

Seymour nodded, and Junior straightened up in surprise.

"What'd she say to you?" he asked.

"She didn't say anything," Seymour said softly. "I just took a close look at her."

"Yeah, well, I can tell you she's into some pretty weird shit."

The image of the puff of wind lifting Emily's skirt away from her belly forced the question.

"Is that all?"

Junior fixed his eyes on him and stared hard.

"Ain't that enough?" he demanded.

"It had better be," Seymour said. "It had just better be."

Just then Eddie Gomez, the night custodian, emerged from the closet. He was about fifty, but his face looked ravaged, and he had a habit of cocking it to one side before he spoke. He cackled and then spat onto the floor.

"Fuckin' place," he said, rubbing the spit into the floor with the toe of his shoe. "Eddie keep it clean." He looked at Seymour and Junior, cackled again, and then shuffled off to the door to the stairway.

Junior's eyes followed Eddie's back.

"That's one sick dude," he said. "I don't know if he's deaf or what. But when you speak to him, he answers like what he just said. Laughs and spits, that's all he's good for. He don't clean nothin' while he's here. I find the place just the same way I left it each day."

"I heard something about him from the landlord," Seymour said, "something about an institution."

Junior laughed a knowing laugh.

"Institution, hell. Yeah, same place I spent some time once. I thought they'd throw the key away on that one. But I'll tell you something, you can't blame the poor fucker. The one time I saw him he had a broken bottle shoved up his ass. He's lucky he's alive, or maybe, seein' how he came out of it, maybe he'd be better off dead."

"Story I heard was he raped some little girl, and they put him away for a long time. He just got out."

Junior nodded.

"I didn't have to hear none of that. I knew he had short eyes. There's only one kind of guy gets treated like he did. Ain't that somethin', he winds up here, sharing a broom with me."

Seymour frowned.

"Yeah, ain't it."

Junior laughed.

"Well, maybe, you know, you've become the patron saint of lost causes."

"Well, let's forget him. You're the one on the other end of the rope around my waist, and you're gettin' too damned heavy to pull up the hill."

Junior began to steer his broom down the corridor.

"I hear you, man, but don't push me. Maybe I gotta cut myself free first." He shook his head as though wrestling with a problem he could not share.

"You mean," Seymour said, "Emily."

Junior waved his hand over his shoulder, then looked back at Seymour.

"You know," he said, "I also feel the rope. But in my case there are two of them."

Seymour untwisted the wire cage that covered the cork in the champagne bottle. He pressed his thumbs against the cork and pushed slowly. When the cork gave against the pressure, he pushed harder and it popped. He put the bottle on the coffee table and caught the bubbling foam in his fingers.

"Tomorrow is liberation day," he said, "but I just couldn't wait." He licked the foam from his fingers and poured out two glasses.

"Are you sure?" she asked.

"About your brother?"

She glanced toward the television set where the numbers of the latest poll showed O'Riley with a clear margin.

"Of course, we already know about the other one."

"As sure as we can be. I got the idea that he's got a problem with Emily."

"I could have told him that."

Seymour shook his head.

"Not quite that way. I think your brother might feel overmatched."

"He didn't say that, did he?"

"Of course not. He wouldn't admit any such thing."

"I want this over. Now."

Seymour pulled her to him.

"And I want you. All the time."

She turned to him, her eyes bright but covered with a fine mist. She settled her body next to his.

"Let's drink our toast now," she said. "To Mr. O'Riley,"
she paused, "and my brother. A happy exit from our lives."

They clinked their glasses together, and she brushed her
lips against his.

"And later, we'll toast again, to us," she whispered.
Seymour leaned over and switched the television off. They
sipped their drinks.

She put her glass down.

"But now it is the night before." She stretched in the
languid motion of a cat rising from a nap and clicked off the
lamp next to the sofa. The room darkened, but he could still
see the outlines of her face, the firm but delicate jut of her
chin, and the way her hair swept behind her ear. He found
her and drew her down next to him.

Later, he could remember no detail. It was like a dream
from which the images had been erased, leaving only the
feeling, and that was so strong in its sweetness that he did
not want to move for fear of losing it. He lay next to her, his
mind racing back over the years they had missed. He closed
the space between them, feeling her legs against his, her head
tucked against his shoulder, and then he closed his eyes.

Four

IN THE PREDAWN LIGHT the city across the river looked like it was being bathed in the mist that rose from the water. The first rays of the sun glinted off windows and metal frames. A tug dragging a garbage scow labored toward the bay. Seymour sat on a bench on the promenade, smoking a cigarette. He waved to a jogger, a young man whose sweaty face, heavy breathing, and uncertain stride suggested the last leg of his run. He did not hear the steps behind him.

"I thought I might find you here," Rosalie said. She leaned over to kiss him. "I hope you're not always going to be this predictable."

"I didn't want to wake you," Seymour said. "I felt too good to sleep any longer."

"Next time, wake me. If you go sneaking off again, I'll have to find a better way to keep you in my bed."

Seymour smiled. It had been a long time since he had been teased, and he gave himself a moment to enjoy the attention.

"I'm going to walk to work, catch Junior first thing, then go to court. I'll call you later when it's done."

She ran her hand through his hair and brought his head down to hers for a kiss.

"Tell my brother that if he acts up, he'll have me to deal with." She smiled, but her voice had an edge.

The walk tired him more than he anticipated, and although the day was cool, he was perspiring when he turned down Smith Street. Heavy traffic crawled toward the bridge and the expressway, thickening the air with exhaust fumes. He watched the commuters in their cars, most of them stone-faced against the frustration, some sipping from a container of coffee as they drove. None were smiling. But he found a spring in his step as he thought of Rosalie and made a mental note to buy another bottle of champagne.

He unlocked the door to his building and entered. In his impatience, it seemed as if the elevator wasn't going to come. His palms were damp, and he felt the blood draining from his head. There was really no reason for Junior not to agree to his petition, even if he wanted to continue working in the building for whatever reason, Emily Levine, or simple perversity. But until it was done, there was always a chance for some slip-up, and he found the thought intolerable.

He took the elevator down to the basement, but when the door slid open he stared into an unlit corridor. He forced himself to take a deep breath. Just because the lights were out, he didn't have to assume a problem. Maybe it was too early for them to be on, but he remembered that they were always on—although he could not begin to imagine what Eddie Gomez did down there by himself during the long nights.

He groped for the light switch and flicked it both ways, but nothing happened. He felt for the overhead bulb. It had been unscrewed, and he tightened it. In the light, he saw the closet door closed. And then he heard a shuffle of feet. His muscles tensed and he flattened himself against the wall, peering down the dimly lit corridor. He recognized Eddie's shuffle even before he heard his spit spatter on the floor.

"Fuckin' bitch," Eddie mumbled. "Who's supposed to clean up now?"

Seymour stepped into his path.

"What's going on?" he asked.

Eddie cocked his head, but continued walking. He seemed to be more bent over than usual, and he was clutching his left forearm with his right hand. Seymour grabbed his shoulder and felt the bone under the thin flesh. Eddie pulled forward for another step, and then stopped. He looked back over his shoulder, down the corridor.

"Bitch," he repeated.

"Where's Junior," Seymour demanded. He grabbed Eddie's right arm, and Eddie shoved him off.

"I ain't cleanin' nothin'," he said with a wave of his hand.

Seymour went to grab him again, but he stopped when he saw the bright red on Eddie's fingers. He recovered himself, but it was too late. Eddie had made his way to the stairs, and disappeared. Seymour walked down the dark corridor. All the lights were out, but he could see a shape on the floor. He looked for another light, but could not find one. He knelt beside the body and flicked his lighter, bringing the flame near the face. Her left eye was open and staring, but the right was puffy and half closed. The blood on her face was dried and rust colored. He expected her to moan when he touched her, but the skin on her neck was cold, and she did not move beneath his hand. He ran the light down her body quickly, knowing before he saw the details what she would look like, how her blouse would be ripped open, her skirt hiked to her hips, and her legs forced apart. But he did not anticipate the wound on her swollen belly, the ragged circle of clotting blood there, still dark red and moist enough on the edges to trickle down her thigh.

His lighter had begun to burn his thumb, so he released the lever, and knelt next to the body. He flicked it back on and brought the flame closer to her neck to confirm what he thought he had seen there, and he had been right: her scarf lay on the floor next to her, and circling her neck was an abrasion, about an inch and a half or two inches wide. He moved the light down her body once more and paused at her right hand lying across her chest. Two of her long, carefully manicured nails were broken.

He struggled to his feet. His mind raced—to Junior, to Eddie, and to O'Riley—and he thought about slipping out of the building through the basement. He forced himself to look at her again. Her other arm was spread out as if it had been pinned. Her rings and bracelets were still there, as were her earrings. Her purse was a few feet away, unopened, and beyond it her coat. It was neatly laid out on the hard floor, almost like a blanket. He took one more look around, walked to the elevator, and rode it up to his office.

"So, Mr. Lipp, tell me how you came to discover the murder."

Detective Rosenberg was a short, grizzled man, with thinning gray hair. He was wearing an ill-fitting suit that hung loosely over his spare frame.

Seymour was about to say that he was on his way to find Junior, but he stopped himself.

"You'll have to excuse me," he said, "I think the whole thing is just hitting me."

Detective Rosenberg looked up from his little notebook, and pointed a stubby pencil at Seymour.

"Sure, take your time Mr. Lipp, but I am curious as to why you were prowling around the basement, for no partic- ular reason. In the dark."

Seymour recognized that it would be stupid to fabricate.

"I was looking for a client," he said simply. The detective raised his eyebrows. "A client," he added, "who works in the building. As a custodian."

Rosenberg nodded.

"Yes, I believe half the city knows your client. Did you happen to find him?"

Seymour stared hard at the detective.

"We're that famous, huh?"

"I'm afraid so, media hype and all that."

Seymour shrugged.

"In any case, no, I did not find him. I did, as I've already told you, run into, and try to restrain, the other custodian."

"Yes," Rosenberg looked down at his notes, "a Mr. Gomez, another ex-con, am I right?"

"Right, straight from upstate."

Rosenberg frowned. "We have here a sensitive case, Mr. Lipp, very sensitive. The wife of a rich man, with heavy political connections through her father, raped and murdered. Maybe she was pregnant."

Seymour realized that the detective had made a couple of assumptions he was not ready to concede, not if, as he suddenly realized, he was to wind up representing Junior in this mess.

"Let's be careful. Do we know she was raped? Or pregnant?"

Detective Rosenberg narrowed his eyes further until he was squinting. Seymour could see that they were slightly bloodshot at the corners.

"That seems fairly obvious, but of course the medical examiner will have to confirm all that. In any case, we know we have a brutal murder on our hands. And you were one of the last people to talk with Mrs. Levine. Is that not right?"

Seymour sighed, and lit a cigarette.

"Yes, or at least I can say that I talked with her briefly late in the afternoon, yesterday, as we were both leaving the building."

"Did you talk about anything in particular."

"Not that I remember." He had decided that he could not, under the circumstances, admit to knowing Emily more than casually, and although that was not exactly true, he rationalized that it was close enough.

Rosenberg's expression did not change.

"She didn't then say anything about being afraid of somebody, or anything like that, or ask you to walk her outside?"

"No, nothing like that."

"Do you have any idea what she would have been doing in the building in the middle of the night?"

"I couldn't say. Maybe it had something to do with her husband's business opening."

"At two or three in the morning? That's the approximate time of death."

Seymour shrugged.

"Well, I'm sure that'll come out, along with everything else." The detective thought for a moment. "Do you know if she had any other particular acquaintances or friends in the building?" He held his pencil poised over his pad.

"Really, detective, I know very little of her personal life. Her husband leased the space upstairs, and she was around a lot while the work was in progress because, as I understand it, her husband was away on business."

"As you understand it?"

Seymour ground out his cigarette.

"Yes, that's how I understand it. That's what it looked like, in any case."

"I see, sir. Is there anything else you can think of?"

Seymour tried to look as though he were concentrating, and then he said, "No, but if I do think of something, I'll let you know right away."

"That would be very good, Mr. Lipp. My number is on my card. In any case, we will be checking out everyone who works in the building. As a matter of procedure, you understand."

"Certainly," Seymour said. "That is your job."

After the detective left, Seymour opened his briefcase and took out the papers he had prepared for Junior.

"Why," he muttered, "couldn't you wait a little bit longer before fucking up?"

He was stretched out on his couch, staring at the faded print on the wall across the room, when the phone rang. He let it ring for a few moments before picking it up. He expected it to be Rosalie, insisting that he let her come over now, saying that she would be there whether he wanted her or not, and he smiled to himself for a second, but he hoped to hear Junior's voice on the other end, calling from God only knew where.

"Lipp, we've got a serious problem. And I expect that you'll handle it with discretion."

Seymour paused to light a cigarette.

"Look, O'Riley. I don't know what you mean 'we' have a problem. Unless you were one of Mrs. Levine's long list of lovers? Or was fat Phil, or her father, a heavy contributor to your campaign?"

"Don't get smart," the prosecutor snapped. "You know perfectly well what I mean. Your boy might take some heat."

"You mean, you might. Let's not forget whose bright idea this whole thing was."

"Him, you, me, all of us, together."

Seymour inhaled deeply.

"You sound as though you know he did it."

"Did he?"

"I sure as hell don't know, but I doubt it. I don't think it would be his style."

"Good. Let's hope you're right."

"But, I've been thinking," Seymour continued, his mind suddenly fixed on the champagne he had not bought, "that if he did, I'd like to watch him burn."

There were a couple of moments of silence on the other end, and then O'Riley's voice sought the right note.

"I'm not altogether shocked to hear you say that," he said. "But we're going a little bit fast. I will, of course, do everything I can to keep him out of this, for as long as I can. Maybe we'll get lucky. I hear there's a good lead to another suspect. Some deranged old bastard."

"I know the gentleman in question."

"I'm sure you do. But not as well as you know your friend, as you've just indicated. So, don't concern yourself. I'll take it from here. All I ask is your cooperation, should it become necessary."

Seymour squeezed the receiver tight.

"I'm going to do my best to find out what happened. As you say, for me it's personal."

"You wouldn't be planning on interfering in police business, now would you?"

"No, just protecting my ass."

He lay on the couch staring at the print on the wall. The lamp was at its lowest setting, but he could see the bearded figures around the plain wooden table on which lay open a scroll illuminated by a single candle, their faces drawn to one who had his finger poised over the text and his mouth half open as though about to speak. Seymour strained for a moment, as though he, too, would hear the pronouncement, but all he heard was the distant rumble of the subway.

The floor shook and the dishes in the cupboards in the kitchen rattled as the F train rumbled up Smith. He waited for the trembling to stop. After a few moments, he realized that it was his body that was shaking. The train had disappeared into the night. He put his feet on the broad floor planks to steady himself, but he could not flush away the image which assaulted him of Junior with Emily, their bodies intertwined on the basement floor. He forced his eyes open to stare at the print on the wall, and again he saw the ancient rabbis looking back at him, impassively, just a slight tremor in their upraised hands.

Seymour heard the knocking on his door and leaned over so that he could read his watch in the light from the lamp.

It was three-thirty. The sour taste in his mouth and the gurgling in his stomach reminded him that he had fallen asleep without eating any dinner. He rolled off the couch and staggered to the door.

"Rosalie, is that you? Just a minute. I'll be right there."

He hurried into the bathroom and splashed water onto his face. He tucked his shirt back into his pants and examined his red eyes and stubbled face in the mirror. He swiped his hair back from his forehead. As he opened the door, he began forming words of apology as to why he hadn't called.

The hallway outside his door was not well lit, and it took him a moment to realize that he was looking at Lois. She stepped across the threshold and pulled his head towards hers for a kiss that tasted of vodka.

"I guess," she whispered, "he's done it good this time. To both of us." Then she laughed, "Sorry to disappoint you, about not being Rosalie, I mean. I won't stay long."

Seymour motioned her into the room, and she sat down on the sofa. He stood before her, trying to force himself awake. She was wearing jeans, running shoes, and a hooded sweatshirt as though she were ready for a morning jog along the promenade or through the park.

"Do you know something I don't?" he asked. "Have you spoken to Junior?"

"No, and no," she replied. "I don't know any more than what I heard on the news about a murder in your building, that plus the fact that he hasn't been home since the day before yesterday."

"Then why did you say he did it?"

"Come on counselor," she laughed. "I'm not some fool on your witness stand. I didn't say he did it. I just suggested that whether he did or didn't, he could have, and that's enough to fix us. Don't you think?"

Seymour nodded.

"It sure as hell doesn't do us any good. Particularly if we can't find him."

"Don't worry. He'll turn up. Just like he always does. And when he does, he'll be looking for your help."

Seymour paced around the room and then sat next to her.

"I've thought about that. And I don't know what I'll do when he asks."

She laughed again, loudly.

"Ask? Since when does he ask about anything?"

"He did once. The time you came to see me."

"That's just the point. *I* came to see you. He would never have done that himself." She studied his face.

"No," she said softly, "that's not why I am here this time. Nothing like that. I wouldn't do that again."

She took out a cigarette and lit it.

"It's like this. I'm the one who needs help now. Even before this, he hasn't been home that much. He's done this trip before. Gets reckless, shacks up with someone some-place for a while. I take him back. Why I can't tell you exactly, anymore than you know why you'll help him. Don't think you won't. But when he's like this, off on his wander-ings, he forgets me, and things like buying groceries. It didn't matter so much before the baby, but now, well, I don't have as many options. To tell you the truth, I don't know what he's been doing with his money for the past couple of months. Maybe he's been playing the ponies, or buying tokens of his affection for Mrs. Levine." She stopped suddenly and ground out her cigarette. She shut her eyes and seemed to drift. Seymour took out his wallet and emptied the few bills he had, no more than thirty or forty dollars. He took her hand and placed the bills in it. She opened her eyes, looked briefly at the money, and then stuffed it in her jeans pocket.

"It's all I have right now. I'll see if I can raise more for you tomorrow."

"No, don't. This'll do me fine. If I hadn't gotten pissed I

wouldn't have come here, and I wouldn't be taking this from you. Think of it," she paused, "as a loan. Or maybe you'd like immediate payment. In services. I've been told I'm good, real good." She settled back on the sofa, her eyes very bright, and he wondered if she had been doing anything more than vodka.

"Really," she whispered. "Don't you remember?" She drew up her sweatshirt up over her head, slowly, pausing with her arms stretched high and her bare breasts revealed. He reached toward them, drawn for the moment into the memory, but the sad flaccidity of the naked flesh dissuaded him, and he grasped the bottom of her shirt and pulled it back down.

"Yes," he said. "I do remember. Just take the money, and forget about it. If you need more, I'll see what I can do."

She pouted for a moment, and then shrugged.

"Maybe there'll come a time when I won't be able to give it away. But not now, not yet. You always were a weird one."

"I guess so," he said.

They sat in silence for a moment, as they had so many years ago after their lovemaking, never knowing how much more time they had, until a knock on the door brought them back to the present, and they stiffened. As though they were teenagers again, they straightened their clothes and smoothed back their hair before Seymour got up to go to the door.

"It's probably Rosalie," he said.

"Well, it's sure as hell not my mother," she said. "She would've used her key."

Seymour opened the door, and Rosalie threw her arms around him and squeezed him to her. He felt himself recoil, just a little, before she was ready. He stepped back and nodded toward Lois who was still sitting on the sofa.

"She was just leaving," he said.

Lois got up slowly and unsteadily. She smoothed her sweatshirt down tightly enough to show the curve of her breasts.

"Sister Rosalie," she said. "Like the man said, I was just on my way out. I'm sure you two have a lot to talk about that doesn't concern me." She walked to the door, but stopped next to them to give Seymour a pecking kiss on the cheek. Then she looked briefly at Rosalie, her eyes hard.

"Remember, Seymour, whatever you might hear, if you want to know about Junior I'm the one who can tell you." She turned again to Rosalie, her face opening to a warm smile.

"You and Seymour must come over some time, for dinner. When this mess blows over."

Rosalie returned the smile.

"Sure, Lois. When, and if, it does."

The two women measured each other for a moment, and then Lois closed the door behind her.

"Please stay, Rosalie."

She was still standing where she had been when Lois left, her hands clenched.

"All I could think about all day was when I should come over here, how I could help you, what I could do, and when I get here, she's leaving like it had been some kind of a party." She fought a sob. "What am I supposed to think?"

"I didn't know she was coming over here. But I wanted to be with you, and at the same time I wanted to be alone. To sort things out."

"Okay." Rosalie whispered, and brought her hand to his lips. "You don't have to explain anything. I know Lois. And I know my brother. I came now because I know you need me. And also because I want to be here when he calls."

Seymour switched the lamp off. Sunlight now bathed the room fully. Rosalie yawned delicately behind her hand. They had been sitting silently on the sofa, huddled against each other like two orphan children. Seymour looked at his watch and stretched back against the sofa.

"I guess I should think about getting ready for work," he said.

She shook her head. "Not today. If you need anything from the office, I'll get it for you. You'll get some rest, and I can be back in an hour. Don't argue. Besides, your most important client is going to contact you here."

"How can you be so sure?"

"He won't go near your office."

"I know that. But maybe he just took off."

"No. He needs you. And he'll get in touch with you. Probably today. And before he does, I want to talk with you about him."

He waited while she collected her thoughts.

"I don't believe," she said slowly, "that he killed that woman."

"I'm not sure I do either," he said. "It really doesn't seem in character. But then, again, how well do I really know him? I have seen him in action."

"Yes, when he was saving your ass."

He drew back at the unexpected bluntness.

"Yes, that," he said, "and stories he's told about taking on a black con who was trying to rape him."

"Did you ever consider that they might be just that?"

"Stories?"

She nodded.

"Why do you think he told you that?"

"I hadn't thought, but I guess, just part of his macho trip."

"Right, but more than that, why tell you, in particular unless he wanted to impress you."

The idea astonished him. It was one explanation that had not occurred to him, but now he remembered the conversation a little more fully, how Junior's eyes had studied his reaction and maybe there had been a little apprehension or even hope behind the mocking smile.

"Didn't you know that he has always wanted your respect, ever since you were kids beating each other up."

Seymour smiled.

"That's more like ever since he used to beat up on me."

"You're forgetting that one time."

"I guess so. There were so many others that went the other way."

"But he never forgot."

"Maybe you're right," he conceded. "But it doesn't make a lot of sense."

She took his hands and searched his eyes.

"Please, trust me. I know I'm right. And you'd better begin to understand it."

He turned the idea over in his mind. All the times he had been unable to explain Junior's behavior and had shrugged his confusion off became just a little clearer if he thought of Junior forcing them into a contest of wills not to establish dominance, as he had always thought, but to gain equality.

"I always figured he had something perverse in his nature, and found me to be a good target to work it out on," he said.

"There's that, too," she replied. "It's all mixed together."

They sat quietly for a few minutes.

"I have to tell you one more thing."

He wanted to deflect any further revelations, and tried to think of something light to say, but she insisted on being heard.

"I lied to you. When you asked about my parents, and I told you how they moved out to the Island. That's only partly true." She looked away for a moment.

"My brother and my father fought, fiercely, for a time."

"About?"

"Not about," she said sharply, "over."

"You're not serious."

She nodded.

"Never more so. Junior knew that our father had his eye on Lois, used to paw her whenever he got the chance. I don't know, maybe it went past pawing and Junior found out, or maybe Lois said something. She's more than capable of that. As you know. Sometimes she wants to hurt and does. I don't know if that was all, but whatever it was it was enough so that my parents did move, suddenly, right after I got married. That part is true, and then I found out that Junior owned the house. And that Lois had moved in with him."

"And now he rents it out?"

"I don't know the details of that, but I think he sold or lost the house to the city." She lowered her eyes for a moment.

Seymour lit a cigarette.

"Is that all?" he asked. He didn't want to hear any more.

"Yes," she answered.

Seymour sat with a cup of coffee, waiting. Rosalie had only been gone for half an hour, but he knew that before she got back, Junior would call. He had just drained his cup when the phone rang.

"Listen carefully," Junior said. "I want to meet with you tonight. Pier 3. At the end of the dock. Midnight."

The phone clicked in Seymour's ear before he could respond.

He watched the taillights of the cab disappear into the mist that thickened beneath the lamppost. Pulling his jacket more tightly around him, he dipped his head into the cold breeze from the river. All he could see was the low slung shape of the building toward which he walked.

He stepped as carefully as he could over the beer cans and bottles that littered the pier. The moon slid behind a cloud, and the light from the street did not penetrate the gloom. When he reached the end of the pier, the breeze stiffened and he felt chilled. He looked down at his watch and saw that he was still a little early. He lit a cigarette and settled down to wait.

It had been more than a half hour. Several times he had walked back to the front of the pier to check that he was at the right place, and each time he had returned to his post with growing concern. What if the police had picked Junior up and were on their way here right now? Or what if the whole meeting had been part of some ploy, and Junior was even now home with Lois, tamping hash into a pipe, both of them laughing their asses off?

He heard a low rumble coming from behind him and he turned toward the building. At first he couldn't see anything, but then he saw the last loading bay door inch up until it was about a foot from the ground. After a moment, Junior's arm snaked out and motioned him toward the door.

The moment he was inside, Junior slid the door closed and lit a candle. He huddled next to it and beckoned Seymour to sit down next to him.

"Cozy little place." He smiled.

"Terrific," Seymour muttered. "I'm frozen."

Seymour thought he saw a brief expression of concern pass over Junior's hard features.

"I'm sorry I had to make you wait, man," he said. "But I had to be sure you weren't followed. Or that you hadn't brought somebody."

"What are you talking about?" Seymour objected. "Why would I do that?"

Junior shrugged. "Just not taking any chances, man, that's all." He took a half-smoked joint from behind his ear and lit it. He inhaled, held the smoke deeply, and offered Seymour a drag.

"Is that what you call being careful?" Seymour said, with a wave of his hand.

"Suit yourself, man. What I said I meant about serious business. Not bullshit like this." He inhaled again, and Seymour held out his hand.

"That's more like it," Junior smiled. "We got to cool out

so we can figure out how you're gonna get me outta this mess."

Seymour hadn't done pot in a long time, and he felt a rush immediately. He handed the joint back to Junior.

"One of us better keep something like a clear head," he said.

"I guess that'll be you counselor. I never was too good that way."

Seymour rubbed his eyes. He would have to ask right off. If he delayed, he might never get a straight answer. Junior, though, was a step ahead.

"No," he said evenly. "I did not do it." He face broke into a broad grin. "Gotcha, that time, counselor. Guess I saved you the trouble of askin'."

"Good," Seymour said. "But the police are going to think that you did. O'Riley would hang you out to dry, except for the moment he might find it inconvenient."

"Then I guess we gotta keep it that way."

"Maybe we can, for a while. But we'll need more than that. A lot more." He shivered, but not from the cold. He felt Junior squeeze his arm.

"I'm right here, babe. Maybe you shouldn't have had that toke."

"It's not that," Seymour replied. "At least, not only."

"Good, I want you thinkin' straight."

Seymour got up, stretched the chill out of his bones, and then sat down again.

"Let's take it from the beginning. You were having an affair with Emily Levine."

Junior nodded.

"You were her pipeline to coke heaven."

"Yeah man, her daddy had all the other faucets shut." He shook his head from side to side. "That man is heavy."

"Yeah, we know that. Too late, maybe for you. And now the best for last," Seymour paused, "she was carrying your baby."

Junior hesitated, and then smiled. "I think so," he said. "What makes you doubt it."

"Nothin' special. You just never know, do you?"

"I think we can take that as a given."

"Whatever you say."

Seymour paused. He hadn't planned this one so soon, but he had to know.

"And then when she found out she was pregnant, she told you to get lost. Right?"

"No, nothin' like that," Junior snapped.

"And you lost your cool. Got rough, right?"

"No, I told you, no way." Junior's voice shook and the veins began to stand out on his neck. Seymour pushed another step.

"Don't give me that bull. I saw her neck, man."

"One more time," Junior whispered. "It wasn't me." Seymour could see that he was about to lose it. He had him set up just right.

"She told you to get lost," he continued. "And you couldn't stand the sting, the insult to your manhood. So you waited for the right time, and then you made sure that she wouldn't dump you. You made very sure. You raped her, and killed her. Slowly, so that her dying memory would be of you."

Junior's arm swung out in a short backhanded arc and his knuckles crashed against Seymour's jaw. Seymour felt his head snap back. He rubbed his bruised chin and fought the urge to strike back. He needed to know more than he wanted to get even, at least for now.

Junior smiled. "Sorry, man. But you been watchin' too many TV shows, or at least the wrong ones. It wasn't that way at all."

"I'm not so sure," Seymour said slowly. "Not sure at all. But you'd better be straight with me or I'm walking out that door, and I'll take my chances alone. Remember who stands to go away for a very long time."

"You're not that clean," Junior snarled. "They'll be lookin' at you. There's plenty of people who can be persuaded to remember how you were trailin' after her, your prick at full mast, dribbling at the thought of gettin' a piece of that rich, kike pussy."

The words bit, and Seymour lashed out. Junior anticipated and ducked his head so that Seymour's fist glanced off his forehead. They grappled and rolled over on the floor. Seymour knew that he was no match for Junior in this kind of fight, but he didn't care. The blood beat in his forehead, and he shoved as hard as he could, his hand against Junior's throat. Junior pushed back against Seymour's chest and they broke apart. They sprang to their feet, and then Seymour saw the gleam of a knife.

"Okay" Junior said. "We both made our points. Didn't we? That's all for the bullshit right now." He snapped the blade closed. "Look we can finish this. Now, or some other time. Or maybe you just want to walk out that door. I won't try to stop you."

Seymour took a deep breath.

"You're right. That other business is old news." His anger flared again. "And we *will* settle it some time."

Junior grinned. "Sure, man. So you had part of it right. I did get rough. Not just once. The bitch was weirded out. Especially when she was high."

"Which was about all the time, from what I saw."

Junior shrugged, as if to say that part of it was beyond his control.

"Like I said, she liked it rough, wanted something around her neck, at first not too tight, not too hard, her scarf, and she'd hold it while she rode me, man, and then one day she put the fuckin' thing around my neck, and I figured what the hell, maybe there was something to this shit."

"And?"

"Nothin' man, nothin. I didn't feel nothin'."
Seymour waited for the last piece.
"Then one day, she asked for my belt. But I didn't off her, man. That's not my style."
"Tell me about it, then. All of it."

He sat alone beneath the promenade, considering Junior's story, both his flat denial, and his admissions—that he had accommodated Emily's taste for the bizarre, that he had met her after work the night she was murdered, that Gomez had surprised them as they lay panting on her outspread coat, and that the crazy old bastard had stood right above them, saliva dripping from his mouth until Junior had shoved him away. Finally, that Emily, deeply humiliated, had insisted he leave her alone while she composed herself, and he had reluctantly agreed, walked the streets for a few minutes, and returned to find her body. It was he who had called the police. This last Seymour found impossible to accept, but Junior insisted. "What was I gonna do man," he had demanded, "she's layin' there cold with my dead baby in her belly and I couldn't even cover her up."

Seymour tried to make Gomez fit that story. He certainly had opportunity. He was there when Seymour arrived hours later, fingers covered with blood. He seemed disturbed enough to be capable of violence, but as for that, Seymour really had seen nothing but a man who aggressively kept to himself. Without a motive, though, the blood on Gomez' fingers did not mean much. He could have tried to move the body, or just touched her to see if she would move, as Seymour himself had done.

He tried Junior's story one more time, wanting to believe it. Junior had admitted that Emily's behavior had begun to make him nervous. But Junior was not stupid, and his anger always seemed controlled, even calculated. He was capable of affection, maybe even love. Would he kill what he loved?

Had he loved Emily, or was she only a toy to engage his darker side, the depths of him where inarticulate promptings moved him like the steady and contrary pull of an undertow?

Far away, a church bell from some lonely spire hidden in the fog tolled four times dully through the damp air. He got up and tried to rub some warmth into his arms and legs. His head ached as though with fever. He took a couple of deep breaths and started to walk toward a telephone booth.

Rosalie did not ask any questions. She picked him up within ten minutes, took him home, and helped him to bed. When he awoke, she was at his side, and he could smell the warmth of a steaming cup of tea.

"I'd rather have coffee," he said without thought.

"This is better for you."

He sipped the tea.

"Do you always have to be right?"

"Most of the time." Her face turned serious. "Are you awake enough to deal with some news?"

He nodded.

"Wait a minute," he said. "What time is it?"

"About noon. I've already been to your office. I figured you wouldn't be getting up for a while. Anyway, I took two phone calls. One from O'Riley and one from a Mr. Goode."

"I know what O'Riley wants. What about the other?"

"Probably worse. It seems Mr. Goode is Emily's father."

Seymour sat up and nodded, slopping the hot tea on his hand and the bed.

"You know him?" she asked.

"Indirectly. What'd he want? How'd he sound?"

"Woa. One at a time." Rosalie sat down next to him and dabbed at the spill with a napkin. Seymour stopped her.

"Never mind that," he said.

She finished soaking up the tea, and crumbled the napkin into a ball.

"It seems," she said, "that Mr. Goode knows a little about Emily and Junior. I don't know how much. But enough." She paused. "He wants to talk to you about his daughter."

Seymour waited.

"He said there was a history there you should know about."

He began to rise from the bed.

"Where do you think you're going?"

"To my office. To call Mr. Goode."

Rosalie leaned over him.

"How are you feeling?"

"Good enough to get up and go to my office and make some phone calls."

"That good?" she smiled, and ran her hand over his chest. "Then why bother getting up?"

"I should at least call Goode," he protested, but she covered his lips with her own.

"Later," she said. "Tomorrow. Anyway, Mr. Goode also mentioned that he would be tied up the rest of the day. Said he'd get back to you."

He pulled her down on top of him.

"Why didn't you say that in the first place?"

They went out for dinner to Angelo's Pizza Palace on Court Street. Angelo's featured three bare, rickety tables with empty napkin holders. Seymour ordered a pie from Vinnie, scooped up a handful of napkins from the pile on the counter, and steered Rosalie to a table in the back.

They ate silently. Rosalie sipped her coke, her eyes searching Seymour's face.

"What's bothering you, babe?" she asked.

He felt the muscles in his neck relax, just a little. He had not realized how much this fragment of thought had been pressing on him. He reached across the table to take her hands, and they sat in silence. After a while, Seymour sat back in his chair, and looked into her eyes.

"I had a thought," he said, "sort of based on what you were telling me."

She stiffened for a moment, her face tense.

"I'm not sure I should have told you those things," she said.

"What I sense is that you have mixed feelings about your brother. That's not so unusual."

Her face darkened.

"Is that all that meant to you?"

"What I meant is that, given your particular brother, I can understand your feelings. I just don't know how far they go."

"Far enough," she said slowly. "He's blood. I love him as a brother, but I fear what's inside of him, the violence."

Seymour nodded.

"That's not quite the whole picture," she continued, an edge to her voice. "I am also attracted to his energy."

"When you say attracted, you mean physically?"

"Yes," she answered, a trace of a blush on her face. "I've read that it's not so rare. When we were little, he'd sometimes carry me to bed, and it felt very, very good, to have his arms around me."

Seymour was silent, not sure if words could serve any more. Yet, somehow, he felt more at ease with her, and suddenly he knew why.

"I think you've just become real for me," he said.

"Warts and all?"

"I'm afraid so."

"Good," she smiled broadly. "Because I've known about yours for a long time. And anyway I had no intention of playing at perfection."

Seymour was at his desk by eight-thirty. Rosalie was going to work half a day, and then join him in the afternoon. He had protested but she was adamant. "After all," she had insisted, "don't you think you can use some help?" He had conceded the point easily. For the first time in a long while, he did not feel alone.

Promptly at ten, O'Riley arrived, accompanied by Detective Rosenberg. The detective looked even more wrinkled than the last time; his eyes were red and swollen. He took out his little notebook and looked toward O'Riley who nodded.

"We'll get right down to business, Lipp. I'm sorry we couldn't get together yesterday. I called you as soon as I received Rosenberg's report. This is now a matter of some urgency." The prosecutor's voice was tense, and his whole manner lacked the ease Seymour had come to expect.

The detective cleared his throat. "We have reliable evidence that Mrs. Levine was having a relationship with Mr. Constantino." He lifted his bleary eyes to Seymour.

Seymour looked over at the district attorney. "O'Riley, can we skip the preliminaries?" He paused long enough to cause the detective to shift uncomfortably from one foot to the other. "And," he continued, "I'm not going to deny the obvious."

O'Riley chuckled. "I'm sorry. We didn't take you for an absolute fool." He turned to Rosenberg. "Just hit the high points."

"As you like, sir. The bottom line is that we think your boy Junior goes to the head of the class. He had a motive, jealousy or some such, it was very probably his baby she was carrying, he had opportunity, and a past history of knife-work. There's more, but those are the highlights." He snapped his notebook closed and put it in his pocket.

Seymour stared at the detective, trying to decide what he would have to concede. At least, Rosenberg hadn't mentioned Junior's dealing.

"Very impressive, detective," he said. "I'm sure, as you say, you have a good deal more to offer us. But in terms of what you have just presented, I don't see much. The only firm tie you've made between my client and this case is his involvement with the victim. Now, granted that does make him a suspect, but I doubt it's enough to indict. For example, do you know the cause of death? Do you have the knife? Any other physical evidence? Fingerprints? A witness who places him anywhere near the scene? Have you spoken to him to see if he has an alibi?"

Detective Rosenberg's face showed just a trace of annoyance. "Now, sir, you know that if we had been able to find him, we would have asked him that very question. But it's like he's disappeared into thin air. And that's not very good for him. It makes us suspicious, when we can't locate a prime suspect." He opened his notebook again, his face now calm. "As for physical evidence, there's quite a bit of that, and we're waiting on the medical examiner's report, of course, but that will take some time." He frowned. "We used to be happy with some blood, fingerprints, what have you. Now they want to start setting up a DNA match."

O'Riley motioned for Rosenberg to stop, and he leaned toward Seymour, a forced smile on his face.

"Now, Lipp, let's stop dancing. If you know where our friend is, I'd advise you to produce him for questioning."

"I'm working on it," Seymour said. He turned to the detective. "Why is it," he asked, "that I don't hear anything about Mr. Gomez?"

Rosenberg began to answer, but O'Riley cut him off. "Because he, too, has disappeared, because he's a less likely candidate, in spite of his record."

"And, most importantly, because you don't expect to see him in your opponent's TV spots as the wanton murderer let loose by a soft-hearted and soft-headed prosecutor," Seymour returned.

"You ought to consider your own reputation, Lipp. Look I'll make it simple for you. This case does not shape up easy. As the detective said, there's a lot of physical evidence. It'll take time to sift through that lot."

"And time is one thing you're short on."

"You'd better believe it." O'Riley's expression, for once, was genuine. "This is all," he said softly, "very unfortunate, for both of us. Maybe I did make a mistake with our friend. It looks that way now. He was going to get into some serious shit, sooner or later."

Seymour nodded.

"I could have told you that, but you weren't listening."

O'Riley cast his eyes toward the ceiling.

"Mea culpa, but now I have to have him in custody. It's as simple as that."

"The way I see it," Seymour said, "you're looking down the barrel. You know damned well, I can slow this thing down."

O'Riley shrugged.

"Okay, Lipp," he said softly. "We'll play it your way for just a little while longer. But let's understand each other. Junior has to surface. If he has an alibi, well and good. Or Mr. Gomez must step forward. If he's the man, good, but I need your friend. Now." He motioned to Rosenberg that they were about to leave, but then he turned back to Seymour. "Just before I came over here, I got a call from Mr. Levine. He wants to know when we're going to apprehend his wife's brutal murderer. And incidentally, he, poor fool, thinks she was carrying his baby. So you can understand his impatience. And her father's."

"We've issued a warrant for your client's arrest," the detective added. "We do want to talk with him. You'd be doing us all a favor if you could get him to come in by himself. Save the taxpayers a lot of money in overtime. But in any case, we'll find him."

O'Riley raised his hand to the detective.

"Come, let's not waste any more of Mr. Lipp's time. I'm sure he has a lot of work to do to find our friend. I believe he is truthful in telling us that he doesn't know his whereabouts, at the moment. A punk like Junior will have enough sense to hide."

They turned to leave, and then the prosecutor motioned Rosenberg to wait outside.

"Do yourself a favor," he said, his eyes hard, "tell us where to find Junior, and then you walk away from this. It's the best thing you can do.

"I took a leave from my job, until the case is over," Rosalie said. Her face, framed by her dark hair, glowed. Her eyes were clear and bright, and her voice admitted no argument. As he accepted this announcement, Seymour realized that what he wanted to do right now was fly off with her to some place warm and sunny, a beach in the Caribbean, perhaps, where they could lie in each other's arms and listen to the gentle surf of the blue ocean waves. With an effort, he brought himself back.

"I guess I'm going to need all the help I can get."

"Thanks a lot," she replied.

"You know what I mean. I have a meeting early this evening, here, with Mr. Goode. When I finally got to talk to him, he was very hush, hush, very discreet. If you want to help, maybe you can see what you can find out about Gomez."

She smiled. "I've already started. I've got his address and I'm going there this afternoon."

"Where did you get the address?"

"From his union. At first, they didn't want to give it to me, but I told them that I was representing an attorney who might have some good news for him."

Seymour chuckled. "They bought that one?"

"Sure they did."

He threw his arms around her.

"You know," he murmured, "we might just win this one." He reflected for a moment. "Whatever that means in this case."

$\triangledown$

Five

MR. GOODE TURNED OUT to be plump and prosperous looking, with a neat mustache and a full head of thick gray hair. His fingernails were manicured and Seymour caught the scent of an expensive cologne as they shook hands.

"I was going to bring Phil with me," he said, "but I think he's too upset at the moment, and who could blame him?"

Seymour took his measure immediately.

"Yes, he's probably not up to the kind of talk we are going to have," he offered.

"I see," Goode said, "that I can get right to the point."

"Please do."

Goode sat down on the chair next to Seymour's desk, reached into his suitcoat pocket, and withdrew a cigar. He lit it, and smiled.

"Would you like one, Mr. Lipp? I assure you they are superb. I have them imported, through various channels. Costs a lot, but good things always do."

Seymour lit a cigarette.

"No thanks," he said. "I'll stay with these."

"Whatever you prefer." Goode sighed. "I see you are a man who trusts his own tastes."

"I try."

"Good. Perhaps that will make our conversation easier. If I can show you how your interests are the same as mine, we will be able to reach an agreement. Don't you think?"

"Perhaps," Seymour said. "But we've already been on opposite sides of the fence once, and maybe that's natural. For us."

Goode looked puzzled, and Seymour prodded.

"I don't suppose you would remember an insignificant landlord/tenant case."

Goode waved his hand in a billow of cigar smoke.

"Never get involved."

"Well, for the record," Seymour said, "you won."

"Of course," Goode smiled. "It's only unfortunate you had to lose." He exhaled a puff of smoke and settled back in his chair. "Well, then," he said, "I hope I can show you how nobody has to lose in this present matter. My interest is simply this. I want my family spared the pain of a prolonged and sensational trial. There have already been unflattering references to Emily's personal life in the newspapers."

"Aren't they true?" Seymour asked.

Goode shrugged.

"That is neither here nor there. That is our private business. But as the matter is of some interest to you, and since you probably know the answer, I will confess that Emily's conduct was occasionally, how shall I say, adventuresome."

"That's one word for it," Seymour replied. "There may be others."

"But that is precisely the point. Of course, there are other ways to describe her behavior, and the newspapers will exhaust the thesaurus in finding them."

"What exactly are you suggesting?"

Goode leaned toward Seymour, and flicked a glowing ember into the ashtray on the desk.

"But I am not suggesting anything. I simply want to deny

the newspapers their gossip." He straightened himself in his chair. "I do not want it known that she was carrying that wop's baby. Surely you can understand that."

Seymour felt as though he had just been slapped. The sudden crudeness of the remark, after the calculated talk that had preceded it, startled him into an awareness that the polished gentleman sitting before him was capable of a quiet, but vicious, violence.

"I can understand your concern, to a point," he said. "but after all, I would have guessed that the important thing for you would be to see her murderer punished."

"Mr. Lipp. My daughter is dead. That is a fact. She was bedding down with scum. That is another fact. I can't change either of those things."

Seymour felt the blood pound in his forehead.

"Sir, that scum, as you call him, is my client."

Goode's face reddened, and his eyes bulged.

"Scum, I say, scum, nevertheless. That the scum is your client does not change what he is."

"Your daughter chose that scum, Mr. Goode. And I can tell you, from my own experience, that if it hadn't been him, it would have been somebody else."

"Like you, for example?"

Seymour shrugged.

"Does that surprise you?"

Goode seemed to relax, and he puffed on his cigar as though a business deal were suddenly turning in his favor.

"Yes, and no," he said behind a cloud of thick smoke.

"Meaning?"

"Let me ask you something, Mr. Lipp. Do you deal drugs?" He paused, for only a second. "Of course, you don't," he continued, "but your client does."

"Did," Seymour said.

"No, does, or at least did, if to nobody else, to Emily." His voice lifted. "He poisoned her, just when I thought we had it licked, when I had managed to shut down all her usual, and some not so usual, sources." Seymour saw the pain thicken Goode's brooding eyes. "I'm sure you understand, that I am a man in a position to do that. Don't trouble yourself trying to figure out how. My daughter was my only child. I wasn't going to see her destroyed."

Seymour felt his hurt, but this was not the time for empathy.

"Emily would hardly have passed for an ingenue."

"Okay," Goode said. "We'll have it your way. No, she was not an innocent. I gave her everything, of course, the old story. And she rebelled, also an old story. But that is not all there was to it."

"Then you'd better tell me, because your song is playing very tired."

"I may have spoiled her," Goode said slowly, "but not for the usual reasons. No, I was trying to make up for what that bastard did to her." For a moment, as Goode passed his hand in front of his face, he seemed lost in a distant thought.

"Excuse me," Seymour said, "but which bastard are we talking about?"

Goode's eyes focused.

"The one who molested her, when she was just twelve, the bastard whose balls I'd like to have in a jar, who is, unfortunately, still alive." He swiped at a drop of moisture in the corner of his eye, but Seymour wasn't sure if its source was anger or grief.

"You must excuse me, Mr. Lipp. But you see, now I have nothing. I had hoped for an heir, my own blood." He closed his eyes for a moment before continuing. "I am old-fashioned. Even if Emily hadn't had her problems, I wanted my grandson—well, you get the idea."

Seymour felt he had to push the sentiment back before he responded to it.

"Now that you are respectable."

Goode nodded wearily.

"Yes, that too. I was not born to wealth, of course. Far from it. I'm sure you know the story. Ellis Island, the Lower East Side, the climb to the top. Not without some scars along the way. But now I am retired. My son-in-law has part of my business."

"The respectable part?"

"You misunderstand, I'm afraid. That's all there is. He does not need to work, God knows, but I wanted to give him something to do."

Seymour understood.

"To help him out. With your daughter."

Goode nodded.

"Yes, he's a good boy, but not too sharp, and he'll be lucky not to blow the whole thing. But that is, as you see, not the point, and anyway maybe I misjudged him. He didn't have to claw his way as I did, and so he looks, in my eyes, soft. Perhaps the clawing is not necessary. Or perhaps his claws are retracted like a cat's. It doesn't matter.

"What does matter is that he is what's left of my Emily and my hopes."

Seymour felt a piece was missing.

"Maybe I can buy that," he said, "but Phil's future, by itself, doesn't cut it. Remember the balls in the jar idea. What happened to that?"

"Yes," Goode began, and then paused. "There is, of course, that. For me."

"But?"

"That is not for her mother. This is too close to the core, Mr. Lipp, so let me just say this. Emily's mother could not, or did not, see the changes in her daughter after the assault. Do you see? I was left to deal with it. By myself."

Seymour thought he could respond, now, a little.

"And you want to let her continue in her," he sought for the right word, one without bite, but Goode saved him the trouble.

"Yes, let her bury the daughter she remembers. I am willing to bury the memories of our daughter with her. For that peace, I am willing to pay a great deal."

Seymour ground out his cigarette. He glanced at the ashtray and saw that there were several half-smoked butts in it.

"Okay. Story time is over. What does all this add up to?"

Goode almost smiled.

"I propose, simply, to remove your client from the spotlight."

Seymour felt his curiosity stir. He disliked Goode intensely, but he didn't have to be suicidal about it. Perhaps this plump little man could offer an acceptable way out.

"Talk to me," he said.

"Good. Let me suggest that you could plea bargain your client. I am in a position to assure you that the deal would be a good one. O'Riley owes me. And in any case, he wants this case shut down in a hurry. A trial will prolong a negative exposure for him."

"He's slippery enough to turn it to his advantage."

"Right you are, but only if he has to. I am sure he'd rather devote his considerable energies to other business."

"I see one serious problem with your proposition, Mr. Goode, in spite of your assurances to the contrary. This is a heinous crime we are talking about. Perhaps a double murder because of the fetus. And good probability of a rape on top of it all. That's quite a package to bargain down."

Goode laughed.

"If that's your concern, put it to rest." His face was smugly confident. "Trust me when I say that even in these circumstances, I can push the right button."

"As far down as manslaughter, no rape?"

Goode did not hesitate.

"Assuredly."

Seymour took a moment to reflect. He believed Goode

could deliver, and he had toyed with the idea himself. He might be able to convince Junior that copping was his best hope. But part of him rebelled at the idea, that part of him that still entertained the possibility of Junior's innocence. And another part hesitated at accepting a deal that would get Junior off if he were guilty.

"My client maintains he is innocent."

"And you believe him?"

"You don't expect an answer to that, I'm sure. But you must know that there is another suspect."

"Of course, but O'Riley doesn't seem too interested."

"Are you?"

Goode's eyes flashed.

"I said I was willing to bury a memory. Not a lie. My people are checking into this Mr. Gomez."

"As I am, you can be sure."

"And I would, too, if I were you," Goode agreed. "Maybe we're beginning to understand each other. I'm hoping that I can count on your cooperation."

"You can count on my doing my job."

"And being reasonable?" Goode urged.

Seymour nodded.

"Fine. I was hoping you would come around. After all, we do share a kinship. My family fled the pogroms and yours the Nazis." He hesitated long enough to light another cigar. "We, too, found a less obvious version of our name."

"That hardly makes us brothers," Seymour snapped. He was incensed at the intrusion, but he also felt the pull, the appeal of shared, therefore somehow diminished, misery.

"No, perhaps it doesn't." Goode's face was hard, but he modulated his voice to a purr. "You don't have to like me, Mr. Lipp, but I can help you." He cast his eyes around the office. "You could be doing a lot better than this."

"I'm satisfied."

Goode narrowed his eyes.

"Maybe you are. For yourself. But I happen to know that your father was not as fortunate as I. He is ill, and I am sure you would want to help him more than you now can."

Seymour shot up from his chair.

"If he wasn't so fortunate," he exploded, "all the more power to him."

"Please remember," Goode said calmly. "I will get what I want, with or without your help. However I need to do it."

Seymour steadied himself.

"Mr. Goode, I am sure that you will do what you want. But you should realize that though I did not grow up on the Lower East Side, I did not grow up easy."

"Yes," Goode replied, "I can see that, and, therefore, I'm sure we'll be able to deal with each other." He reached into his jacket pocket. "Here, take a cigar. It might help you to reflect." He laid a cigar on the desk, and Seymour picked it up.

Goode turned on his heel and left. Seymour sniffed the cigar appreciatively, and then crumbled it into the wastebasket.

Rosalie and Seymour got out of the car service car on the corner nearest the entrance to the housing project on Flushing Avenue.

"Remember, buddy, pick us up right here, in one hour, exactly. Got it?" Seymour handed the fare to the driver who bobbed his head in reply.

"If you're on time," Seymour said, "I'll take care of you."

The driver flashed a toothy smile.

"No problem. I be here."

"Maybe yes, probably no," Seymour said.

"So little faith in human nature?" Rosalie asked.

"I'm sure he wants to come back to pick us up, and he probably believes that he will, but from the size of his pupils, I wouldn't give him better than even money."

The project's buildings were utilitarian rectangles, no ornament or curve to soften their hard lines. A number of the windows were visibly broken, others boarded up. The ones that were intact were covered, for the most part, with cheap shades. Some had no covering, and residents could be seen walking from room to room or sitting before televisions. Brown grass showed through cracks in the walkways between the buildings. Wooden benches lined the walks at even intervals. Most had slats missing and all had been spray-painted in luminescent colors that glowed in the moonlight. Groups of teenagers congregated beneath the lampposts listening and dancing to music blaring from ghetto blasters. Shadowy figures could be seen in twos and threes conducting business in corners away from the light.

"This place didn't look anything like this this afternoon," Rosalie said. "I didn't notice the paint on the benches, and the only people around were some old folks walking with shopping carts."

"You must have hit a down time," Seymour replied.

"I guess so. In any case, Gomez' building, I think, is right around the next corner."

"Let's hope we have better luck this time."

"I'm not sure if anybody was home. I thought I heard some noise from inside the apartment. But nobody would answer the door."

"Do you have any idea who would be home?" Seymour asked. "Besides Eddie himself?"

"No," Rosalie answered. "But by the way I am curious. What are you going to do if Eddie answers the door?"

"I haven't really figured that one out. At the least, I can ask him about finding the body, try to corroborate Junior's story. I don't really expect him to give us any useful answers. I guess I'm hoping that some other family member will be there. Hey," he smiled, "I'm no Perry Mason. I'm just making this up as we go. Now, if Mr. Gomez were being evicted, then I'd be on firmer ground."

They were in front of Gomez's building, but neither made a motion to go in.

"It's possible," she said slowly, "that we might find out something neither of us wants to know."

Seymour studied the tension around her lips.

"Not likely," he said.

"But we might. So there's something I want to tell you first."

Seymour glanced around, knowing they should not stand still for much longer.

"Can it wait?"

"No," she said firmly. "And it's probably not what you're thinking. But, I'll make it quick. You see, I knew about him and Emily almost from the start, and I didn't want you mixed up with him. Or her."

Seymour started.

"Her? You thought I might be involved with Emily Levine?"

"Is that so far fetched?"

"No," he said slowly. "Not at all."

"I wouldn't have let that happen. Anyway, I told Junior he was looking for trouble, but he just laughed, like he always does."

Seymour knew they should go in. Out of the corner of his eye, he saw a band of teenagers ambling toward them. But he took a second to sort through what she was saying.

"I'm not sure what you mean," he said. "What do you mean you wouldn't let it happen."

Her voice hardened a little.

"I'm not exactly sure what I mean, either, but those are my feelings."

The teenagers now were within ten feet of them, and Seymour pushed Rosalie through the door.

"Which floor?" he asked.

"Third."

"We'll take the stairs."

The woman's eyes wore the look of an animal that has just escaped a snare. They darted from Seymour to Rosalie, and then searched beyond them.

"Eddie not home," she said.

"Could we just talk with you a moment," Seymour said as soothingly as he could. He handed her his business card.

"I don't read so good," she said, and thrust the card into her apron pocket.

"I'm a lawyer working on a case. This is my assistant. Maybe you can help us."

"Don't know nothin' about no case. Eddie not home. Come back later." She started to close the door, but Seymour put his weight against it.

"Please," he said. "This won't take very long. You know that Eddie is not going to be able to tell us much."

"Hmm, that bum," she sneered. "Come on in."

She stepped aside and Seymour and Rosalie walked into the apartment. They found themselves in a sparsely furnished living room, dominated by a large color television on top of which sat a VCR. A game show with contestants trying to guess famous headlines was on. The woman lowered the volume but did not turn the set off.

"Eddie bring that home one month ago," she said. "I don't know where he got the money."

She sat on the sofa, her eyes shifting from Seymour to Rosalie. There were no other chairs in the room.

"How are you related to Eddie?" Seymour asked.

She turned her head to the television screen before answering. She seemed to be concentrating on the clues being flashed before the contestants.

Seymour began to repeat the question, but she snapped her reply while still looking at the screen.

"What you think? He's my man."

"Does Eddie have any sisters? Brothers?"

She wheeled her head around on her plump neck as deliberately as a tortoise emerging from its shell.

"He have only me," she said. "Nobody else."

Seymour looked at Rosalie and shrugged.

"Let me try," she whispered.

"You no have to try hiding from me," the woman said. "I hear good. Everything that crazy bastard say when he don't think I can hear, I hear. He go around talking beneath his breath but I know what he say."

"And what is that?" Rosalie asked.

"Crazy stuff. Always crazy stuff."

"Does he ever talk about his job?"

The woman cackled.

"His job? Sure. He go around like this." She got up and moved her arms as though she were pushing a broom. And then she spat on the floor.

"Yes," Seymour said. "But what does he say?"

"One time," she said, her eyes steady, "he talk about, I think, a woman. On the floor."

"Anything else about this woman?" Seymour asked.

She had turned back to the television.

"No, nothing. I don't know what he talking about." She cackled again. "Eddie, he don't know nothin' about no woman."

Seymour walked over to her and handed her another card.

"If you remember anything else, please give me a call. Any time. Day or night. My home number is right on the card."

"Sure, if I remember anything." She shoved the card again into her apron pocket, and looked at the television, her brows furrowed.

"Russians Launch Sputnik," she said loudly, just before one of the contestants.

They took the elevator down, but although Seymour was sure that he had punched the button for the first floor, the car creaked down to the basement. Seymour was about to push the button again when he saw a figure crouched in the shadows.

"Wait here," he said to Rosalie.

"No."

He heard footsteps coming toward them. He looked toward where the figure had been, and he could just make out the gaunt shape and a flash of white on the arm. The steps quickened, and he leaned hard on the button.

Seymour sat at his desk reviewing the notes he had been making. He heard the door open, and Rosalie, carrying a manila envelope, hurried in. Her face was flushed.

"I was just thinking," he said, "that I remember less than I thought about criminal law."

She tossed the envelope on his desk.

"Forget that, for a moment. You'd better read this."

He reached for the folder, but she was too impatient.

"I checked on Gomez, who is not Gomez, at least he wasn't until recently."

He pulled a pile of copies of newspaper stories out of the envelope. She stopped him.

"There's more."

He sat back.

"Okay. I'll read this stuff later."

She reddened.

"I'm sorry. But listen. That story about Emily being molested. Well, something did happen."

"Was she?"

"That's the point. It's not clear." She reached into the pile of papers and withdrew one. "Here, look, there was a trial, of one," she scanned the print, "of an 'Eduardo Rodriguez,' accused, and ultimately convicted, of sexual assault of one Emily Goode," she paused, "age twelve."

"No shit," he muttered, "I didn't really buy that story."

"Maybe you shouldn't have."

"Huh?"

"Because, it's all there, you'll see, the case was unclear. Rodriguez kept claiming he hadn't done it. He worked for Goode, as a gardener, I think, and little Emily was his buddy, until one day she told Daddy a story, a very confused one, about being attacked, but the details did not seem to add up very well, and the police had serious doubts, particularly because she offered the story after she had been caught sneaking out at night. To meet some friends, she said, but Goode thought it was a particular friend."

"Rodriguez?"

"That's what Goode concluded, but very possibly a neighborhood kid, just up the block, whose parents left him alone a good deal of the time like when they were off on a cruise. He was seventeen anyway."

He finished for her.

"And Goode wasn't having any of that, and so he pushed hard, and got a confession, lesser charge, but serious enough to send him away for a long time."

Her face darkened with concern.

"There's one more thing on that point. The family lawyer, for Goode, well, there's no easy way. You know him. Or did."

Seymour sat back as though a heavy hand had pushed against his shoulder.

"He told me he had once been in the same kind of box. But I had no idea. Screw it. That's history. Along with a lot of other shit. What else do you have?"

"I'm sorry," she said.

"History is filled with clay feet." But he knew that he would have to deal with this one at another time.

"Should I go on?" she asked, and he nodded.

"Just this, it's there on the bottom of the pile, the most recent clipping, just a little story, really, that Rodriguez was recently paroled, and that he changed his name."

Seymour shuffled through his papers.

"It says he had been transferred, after repeated assaults on him by other convicts, to another prison, way the hell away."

"And became?"

Seymour scanned the article.

"Mr. Eddie Gomez, paroled last month, his prison psychiatrist offering the judgment that he had recovered from his assorted traumas."

"When did you say you got that call from a parole officer?"

"Just about a month ago," Seymour said. He stood up and hugged her.

"This might explain a lot of things."

"Like why he acted crazy."

"Acted is maybe right. Waiting for his moment of payback—after all those years."

Rosalie frowned in disbelief.

"I have trouble with that one."

Seymour nodded.

"So do I. And why he was hiding in his own damned basement, if that was him."

She seemed lost in thought for a moment, and then she said very slowly, "Still, it's possible that my brother is innocent, after all."

"Didn't you say," Seymour demanded, "that you believed he was?"

"Yes," she said. "But that was more an act of faith. Now I have reason."

Seymour paced the floor nervously, and lit a cigarette. He felt it was time to give voice to his own deepest concerns, as if in the speaking he would be able to confront them.

"As Junior's attorney, I have assumed that he is innocent. Given what I know of him, I have not been able to decide whether he is. I'm trying to keep the two things separate. I'm defending him as an innocent man. If I had reason to believe him guilty, as his attorney, I would still have to defend him as best I could."

Rosalie walked over to him, and smiled.

"And what does all that mean?" she asked.

"It means," he said, "that we'll check this Gomez thing out very carefully. Maybe go back and try to find him in his hole."

O'Riley called as soon as Seymour walked into his office the next day.

"Have you heard from our chap?" the prosecutor asked.

"Not a word," Seymour answered.

"You know, Rosenberg will find him."

"I'm hoping to be able to bring him in under his own steam."

"One way or the other. But I have to do something. My opponent has restrained himself, so far, perhaps out of a sense of decency, but more probably because his media people haven't come up with something nasty enough yet." He paused. "I have to keep a step ahead, so I'm going to announce our chap's place at the top of the suspect list tomorrow."

"What's the point? We all know that already." Seymour knew the answer, but he wanted O'Riley to say it. The prosecutor did not disappoint him.

"What we know is meaningless. What the public knows is the important thing. You know that, Lipp. Don't pretend that you are unaware of the rules of the game. Not at this stage."

"Of course, I do," Seymour said. "That's why I'm going to suggest something to you. I've seen the headlines, wondering when the city was going to apprehend the vicious murderer. You know it's sort of like the Colosseum, and it's our job to toss somebody, it doesn't matter who, to the lions. Am I right?"

"I wouldn't put it so crudely," O'Riley said. "But yes, in substance, that is correct."

"I thought so. Well, since it doesn't matter who the meat is, if you can give me a little time, maybe I can serve up Gomez."

O'Riley snorted into the phone, "Not that one again. Please spare me. The man is mentally incompetent. I know Goode mentioned that to you, but I am not sure anyone will buy it."

"The lions won't care. But more than that, I have reason to believe Gomez might be the man."

"Tell me about it." O'Riley's tone indicated that he was genuinely interested.

"In time, but I want to be sure, first."

"You've got a day, two at most. Meanwhile I'll put Rosenberg on that one, too. But the poor man can do just so much by himself."

"He's good," Seymour offered, "but surely he's not a one man show."

"You'd be surprised," O'Riley answered, "at the drop off after him. Have you seen my spot?"

Seymour took a second to follow the jump.

"No, I'm afraid I've been too busy."

"Well, catch it some time. Better, I'll send you a copy. You do have a VCR, don't you?"

"No."

"No matter," O'Riley continued, sounding now somewhat manic. "I'll send it over with a player. When you see it, you'll understand how my opponent has let the mayor castrate the department."

"I'll look forward to it," Seymour said.

"Twenty-four hours, then our chap's picture hits the front page."

The phone clicked, and Seymour could imagine O'Riley in the robes of Pontius Pilate, looking down from his throne, and with elaborate gestures, showing that he was washing his hands of the whole matter, or if not that, ready to rectify the mistake he had made in the interest of trying to help a hardened criminal. But, Seymour knew, the prosecutor would be just as happy showing the howling crowd Gomez' head.

He had bought a little time, not much, but it would have to do. After O'Riley's call, he started interviewing the other people in the building, hoping that somebody would give him just a crumb of information about Gomez. He talked to the salespeople and manager of Phil's Fur Salon, but came up empty. Most of them didn't want to talk about the case. A cashier, a young and decidedly plain woman, was more than happy to share her suspicions that the wife of her boss had been carrying on with just about every man in the building, Seymour excepted, because he was standing right in front of her. He thanked her for her information.

"I hope I've been helpful," she said coyly. "I've never done anything like this before. I was becoming embarrassed working here, you know." She paused long enough to shove her gun into her cheek with her tongue. "I mean, I like to be respectable." She seemed perplexed for a moment, and then added, "Let me know if I can help you again." Her smile revealed a shard of gum on her incisor.

"Here's my card," Seymour said. "If you remember anything else, please get in touch. Particularly, anything about the custodians."

"Geez, we didn't see much of them." Her face brightened. "But that one, dark-haired guy, he was kind of cute. And now I think of it, I kind of remember him hanging around with Mrs. Levine quite a lot."

"What about the other one, the night custodian?"

She shuddered.

"I saw him once, when I was late because I had trouble closing my register, it must have been when I had just started, but that was enough."

"Was he doing anything unusual?"

"Just pushing his broom, but his eyes, well, you know what I mean."

"Thanks," Seymour said. "You've been more than helpful."

Apparently, either nobody knew anything more than he did, or if they did they were reluctant to talk. He picked up various attitudes about Junior, ranging from respect to complete mistrust. Some thought he was hardworking, others that he looked like "he had a past," which made them nervous, and a few made smirking references to Emily. People had even less to say about Eddie. The consensus was that he was crazy and that was all there was to it. But one person, an ambitious young salesman who dreamed someday of opening his own, high-class fur salon and who openly disdained Phil's discount operation as inappropriate, offered a nugget of information.

"I do remember one thing," he said just as Seymour was about to wish him good luck in his store, if and when he ever opened it, "once I saw Mrs. Levine talking to that strange custodian. Like I told you, I come in early and leave late. Want to learn as much as I can about this business so I can get outta here and start my own. Anyway, once, maybe twice, I saw those two together. It looked like they were arguing. His eyes opened in wonder. "Say," he said, "you don't think he might have done it, do you?"

Seymour fought to maintain his composure. He hadn't expected anything from these interviews, certainly not from the pale young man in front of him who looked as though he hadn't been out in the sun in years, and whose dull eyes seemed lost in the yellow flesh of his face. But just maybe he had stumbled onto the break that would provide something concrete to hand to O'Riley.

"What else can you remember? About that time?" he asked.

The young man's response came without hesitation.

"I'm afraid that's about it," he said.

Seymour felt a rush of anger.

"You mean, all you can tell me is that you saw Mrs. Levine and Eddie Gomez talking?"

"That's about it. I said it didn't seem like much. Not so much that they were talking, but the way she looked later."

"The way?" Seymour prodded. Does this guy know something or not, he wondered. "What about the way?"

"Scared," he said simply, "like she had seen something she never wanted to see again."

"Did you ever hear anything they said?"

The young man's face reddened.

"Oh, of course not. I didn't want her to think I was snooping around. But I guess I can't hurt her with what I know any more."

"Which is?"

The salesman looked blank.

"What is it you know?" Seymour said, forcing himself to be calm.

"What I told you. About the argument, and how she looked."

"When did you say this conversation took place?"

His eyes brightened.

"What? Are you trying to catch me up? I didn't say. But I think it was about a week or so ago, right before she got killed.

"What do you think?" Seymour asked. "It's beginning to look possible."

Rosalie sipped her wine, and then shoved aside their dinner plates to make more room for her glass. She found a wet spot on the table and drew circles in it for a moment before wiping it up with a napkin.

"I was thinking," she said, "this is all too convenient."

"I know. Somehow I was hoping you wouldn't see it the same way. But right after O'Riley shows interest in Gomez as a replacement suspect up pops this salesman, just about the last one on my list to interview, and hands us a lead in that direction. And then before I have a chance to consider that one, who calls but that Gomez woman, Esmeralda she called herself, wanting to speak to me again. Seems she remembered something."

"Still," she murmured, "it could all be legitimate." Her face was drawn.

"I'll go to Gomez's place again."

"Tomorrow," she said.

"I thought I'd just look over your notes and the clippings one more time. See if I missed anything."

"Tomorrow," she said. "It'll all still be there."

They had just fallen asleep, Rosalie lying with her head on his shoulder, when the phone rang. He reached to the night table and swatted at the alarm clock, but the ringing continued. His body lingered in the languor of his exhaustion and the touch of her flesh, but he groped for the phone. When he heard the voice, he lifted himself up and tried to get his mind to work.

"Later, tonight. It's gotta be tonight," Junior said. "Don't argue, and don't ask questions. I've got the word that things are going to break soon. We have to talk. Just listen. I'll tell you where and when."

Seymour found a piece of paper, scribbled the address, and then put the phone down. He fumbled for his cigarettes and lit one. Rosalie turned on the light. She propped her head on her hand and forced a smile.

"What'd I tell you. When you've forgotten him, he turns up. Don't tell me. You're meeting him tonight."

Seymour nodded.

"He didn't leave me a lot of choice. Hung up before I could

say anything." He studied the piece of paper and then handed it to her. "Hold onto this, just in case."

"Then, you'd better get ready," she said. "Tomorrow came a little early thanks to Junior. How much time do you have?"

"I'm meeting him in an hour."

"Be careful," she said. "I'll wait up."

"I might be very late."

"I'll be up," she insisted. "What do you think?"

"I think," he said, "that you will do precisely as you please. And," he paused, "I wouldn't have it any other way."

Even though it was after two when Seymour got out of the cab on Avenue D, there were still a few people on the street. He saw a couple, walking unsteadily, arms linked, halfway down the block. They passed under a streetlight and he could make out that they were both young men. As Junior had instructed, he walked two blocks until he found The Sitar, a tiny restaurant on the edge of an alley. A dark-looking man in a shabby raincoat stumbled out of the restaurant and staggered by him. Seymour waited until he passed, and for a moment their eyes met. When he was gone, Seymour turned down the alley and walked to the back of the building. He waited a few minutes, and then lit a cigarette. A light flashed on in the back window of the second floor, as promised, and he made his way toward it. He found a door ajar and pushed it open.

He was inside the back entrance to the building, facing stairs that led up to the second floor. Apparently, there was an apartment to the right of the stairs because he could see light beneath another door, and he heard low voices and then a woman's laugh. He paused for a moment, and then started up the stairs. The only light came from a bulb on the landing, and he almost tripped over the figure huddled near the top of the stairs. It was the same man in the raincoat, and this time his movements were quick and purposeful. He sprang to his feet and turned Seymour against the wall. He ran his hands along Seymour's sides and then down his legs, and before Seymour had a chance to react the man was down the stairs.

"That's okay, Pedro," Junior called from the doorway on the second floor. "You didn't have to frisk him."

Seymour glanced up at Junior and then down the stairs where the man had sat down again. He could just make out a smile from the dark face. He walked down a couple of steps to make sure. He got close enough to the man to check out the gold front tooth.

"It's a new one, man," Pedro grinned.

Seymour rubbed his knuckles.

"I've still got the old one, at home in a box."

The smile faded from Pedro's face.

"Hey, man, that was an accident," he said. "Next time will be different."

Junior was at Seymour's side.

"I told you about that," he said. "There ain't gonna be any next time."

"Sure, sure." Pedro half snarled, half smiled. "But just in case there is."

Junior took Seymour's arm.

"Small world," he said. "But he's very useful. Very good."

They went up the stairs and into the apartment, which turned out to be one room furnished with a bed, a cheap wooden night table, and a lamp covered with a dirty and torn shade.

"What would have happened if I hadn't lit that cigarette?" Seymour asked.

"He would've cut you," Junior smiled.

"It's a good thing you didn't ask me to whistle."

Junior waited, and then Seymour added, "I can't. And where would you be without your counselor?"

"But I know you can smoke, man," Junior laughed. "So no problem. You know you should give that shit up. It's no good for you." He swept his arm around the room. "How do you like the place?"

"It looks adequate," Seymour answered.

"That's what it is." He paused for effect. "Lois used to bring her johns here. Pick them up in the village, mostly suburban types, and stroll them down here to the low-rent district. I kind of kept my interest in the place. You never know when you might need somewhere to disappear."

Seymour tried not to picture it. Lois, arm in arm with a young businessman, his eyes lit with lust and hers laughing while her hand sought the inside of his thigh. And in bed, in the room below, she offered him her breasts, and when they were through he plucked his wallet from the inside pocket of his neatly folded suit jacket and handed her a bill. Seymour had to force his attention back to Junior.

"It's time you surfaced," he said. "In a day, your face will be all over the front pages of every newspaper."

A woman's moans drifted up from the apartment he had passed, and he started.

Junior laughed.

"Take it easy, man," he said. "That ain't Lois. She's home with the baby." He furrowed his brows. "Maybe that's not what's bothering you. Maybe you'd like some of that, huh? Am I right? I'll tell Pedro to set it up for when we're done. On the house."

"I don't think so," Seymour said slowly. "But just tell me one thing. Is she working for you?"

Junior's face beamed.

"No, she's just a friend. I got a lotta friends, you know? From the old days before I became respectable."

"When was that?"

Junior looked confused, for a moment, and Seymour smiled.

"Just when did you become respectable?" he insisted.

"You should know that better than anybody." Junior's

manner changed, and Seymour made a mental note of the sensitive spot. "Anyway," Junior continued. "If you don't want no pussy, I guess we should get down to business."

The sound of a slap, flesh against flesh, now reached them, and then the thud of something solid against the wall.

"Getting a little rough for your friend," Seymour said.

"No sweat. Kitten can handle it. And, anyway, Pedro is looking out for her."

"A man of many talents."

"Like I said, he's useful. Now, let's get down to it. But I'll tell you right off, that I ain't showing myself unless you got something very good to offer."

"I don't know how good it'll be. But on the other hand, I don't know how the idea of jail strikes you. If we don't do something damned soon, that's where you'll be heading. You might go there anyway, for a while."

"Not unless they catch me."

Seymour had expected this reaction.

"They will. You can bet on it. Our friend, O'Riley, has a serious interest in this case. And he's put a damned good detective on it. He'll sniff you out. Sooner or later."

Junior looked pleased.

"I'm that important, huh? Probably their best fuckin' man out lookin' for me."

"I'm disappointed in you," Seymour answered. "You sound like a cheap hood who doesn't know which end is up. What difference does it make who catches you. The thing is, you'll be caught, whether it's Dick Tracy or the Lone Ranger, doesn't make any difference. What does make a difference is how you wind up in their hands. If we walk in, maybe we can deal. If not, it's their play."

"Deal," Junior snapped. "Who said anything about dealin'? I don't like the sound of that. You sayin' I should cop?"

"Maybe," Seymour said softly. "But let's take it one step at a time."

Junior's hand shot out and grabbed Seymour's collar and twisted.

"The first step," he said, "is to understand that I ain't coppin' for something I didn't do." He relaxed his hand without removing it, and smiled. "That's one of my principles."

Seymour brought his forearm up sharply and knocked Junior's hand away.

"And my first rule is never to talk to a client who's got his hands on my neck."

Junior threw his head back and laughed.

"When you're right, you're right. Like I always say. But don't talk to me about a plea."

Seymour leaned towards him and fastened his eyes on his.

"I'm not saying you should. But we'd better keep it as an option unless you can give me something to go on, more than what I have now."

"Which is?"

"On the down side, I have a client who the whole world knows was sleeping with the victim, a client who disappeared right after the murder, a client with a record, not a spectacular one, mind you, but one long enough and interesting enough to make it hard to form a defense based on character references. Further, my client had motive—a sexual relationship that seemed to be souring—and opportunity. Plus, he was dealing."

"Hey, man, whose side are you on?" For the first time, Seymour detected a note of concern in Junior's voice, and just a shadow of doubt in the confident eyes.

"I'm just telling you what we're up against. What I have to work with on the plus side is the possibility that Eddie Gomez might have reason, vengeance, to kill Mrs. Levine, crazy as that sounds. That, plus the intention of both the prosecutor and her father to get this case out of the newspapers as quickly as possible."

Junior's eyes narrowed in thought.

"Yeah, Emily told me something about that."

"About what?" Seymour demanded.

"About how her father never did give a good shit about her or anything but what he called the family honor. And that thing about Eddie. I didn't believe her when she told me that the creep was bothering her. I thought she was just blowin' steam, you know, to see what I'd do, and so I just laughed in her face."

"Maybe you should have taken her seriously. If what Rosalie has turned up checks out, Eddie was looking for her for a long time."

Junior did not hesitate.

"Naw, man. I told you about her. She was always sayin' crazy things, but" he paused, "she sure was scared of him." He shrugged. "No help, now."

"I guess not," Seymour said. "You're just remembering all this stuff now? You didn't mention it before."

"No, man, I just forgot. How many times I gotta tell you. You can trust me. Shit, we're fuckin' with my life now. This is serious business."

"I'd like to believe all that."

"You can. Trust me." Junior's tone was sincere, and Seymour decided that he would. He didn't really have any choice.

"Tell me what you know about Gomez."

"First thing, I never bought the dude's act. Even with what I know he went through. Nobody that crazy would still be walkin' around. Don't get me wrong. He ain't right, that's for sure, but he's more right than he looks like."

"Maybe so," Seymour conceded. "This salesman who worked in the showroom claimed he saw some kind of argument between Emily and Gomez. Do you know anything about that?"

"No, but maybe something better will turn up," Junior smiled. "You never know."

Seymour sat up straight.

"Don't get any ideas," he said. "You keep your nose, and Pedro's or anybody else's, the hell out of this. Tomorrow morning I want to walk you into the police station."

Junior shot to his feet and paced around the room. He stopped in front of Seymour, his dark eyes alive.

"That's the way it's gotta fall," he said. "What are my choices?"

"Only one. If you hide, they will eventually catch you. If you turn yourself in, we can try to keep our options open."

"You mean like a plea."

Seymour nodded.

"If it comes to that. Would you rather go away for a very long time? We're talking double murder here, and rape of a pregnant woman. I'd say," Seymour pretended to calculate, "at least twenty years before a chance of parole."

Junior shuddered.

"Twenty years. I won't do twenty days. You know what happened last time. That was no bull." He sat down next to Seymour and turned him by the shoulders so that their faces were inches apart. "You ever been ass-fucked? Ever been held down while some guy shoved it into you?" He squeezed Seymour's shoulders. "It ain't gonna happen again."

"Forget the plea bargain for a second. That's last ditch. I'm not sure how far we can go with that, anyway. But if you turn yourself in, at least it'll buy me some more time. To track down this Gomez thing."

Junior sat back in silence for a few moments.

"Okay. I guess I'll have to go with it." He paused. "You gotta promise me one thing, though."

Seymour waited.

Junior took a breath.

"I want you to take care of Lois while I'm in the cage."

"I'll do what I can, of course," Seymour said.

"You're surprised, huh?"

"You're reading my mind."

"You think I don't care what happens to her, I know, but, Jesus man, you should know better." He pounded his fist against the arm of the sofa hard enough to make it shudder. "I thought you would understand by now. Just make sure nothin' happens to her. That's very important to me. When I'm not around, there's no tellin' what she's gonna do."

"You got it," Seymour said.

Junior relaxed and took out a cigarette.

"Relax," he said. "This one comes from a regular pack." He lit the cigarette and inhaled. A smile began to form around his lips. "A little while ago, you said something about Rosalie?"

"What of it?"

"Nothin', just that it's nice to know that my loyal sister is helping us out."

"She thinks you're innocent."

"Blood is blood," Junior said simply. He shook another cigarette out of the pack and offered it to Seymour. Seymour was about to light it when angry shouts jumped up from the apartment below. He lit the cigarette and listened. Junior was on his feet, standing by the door, his body tensed for flight. It was quiet for a moment, but then there was a scream, high pitched, the sound of bodies struggling against each other, and then a thud. A second later, Pedro raced into the room.

"A bad scene, man," he said. "I hadda waste the john. He was into some weird stuff, and it was, like, getting out of hand."

Junior nodded, as though, Seymour thought, he were a corporate executive being told the details of a merger.

"I'd better blow," he said to Seymour. "All of us."

Seymour got up and walked to the door.

"What about Kitten?" he asked.

Junior's face darkened.

"Yeah, we gotta do somethin'. We'll get her out and take her along."

"She's okay," Pedro smiled, his gold tooth bright in the dim doorway. "I got her untied. Just a couple of bruises. She'll make it out herself and be workin' again tomorrow."

Junior took Seymour's hand as they stood in the alley behind the building. Lights were on in windows across the street.

"We don't have time, now. I'll call you tomorrow. If I can. If you don't hear from me, you just go in and buy us some time. I'll show."

Seymour nodded.

"Make sure you do."

He caught the first stab of the whirling red light about a block away. Junior had already taken a step into the darkness.

"I'll call," he said. And then he was gone.

Seymour knew he should run, too, but he took a second to clear his mind. As they had lept down the stairs, he had stopped in front of the first floor apartment. The man, nude, was on the floor where he had fallen face down, his neck slit, blood puddled around his head. The woman still had pieces of rope tied to her arms and legs as she struggled into her clothes. Her hands were covered with blood, but Seymour didn't know whose. Strands of rope were also on the four corners of the bed. The room had been dark, but Seymour had been able to see her face well enough to make out the puffy lips and swollen eyes. She had taken a step toward them, almost fallen, and clutched Junior's arm to steady herself. Junior had swiped at the blood on his sleeve as she recovered her balance and stumbled out of the room and into the darkness outside.

Seymour heard a car door slam, and he saw Pedro supporting Kitten as they stumbled down the street. He swung himself over a rickety wooden face into a backyard behind another building, and walked silently in the shadows of an alley until he emerged into a quiet street.

$\triangledown$

Six

Rosalie opened the door for Seymour before he had a chance to put his key in the lock. She was wearing one of his white dress shirts, and the olive skin of her thighs and chest glowed. Seymour embraced her and ran his hands under the shirt and over her bare buttocks. For a moment he let himself forget.

"Problem?" she asked.

"You might say."

She took his arm and led the way into the kitchen. She poured a cup of tea from the pot on the table.

"Want one? There's semifresh coffee ready, too."

"I'll have the coffee. Haven't you gotten any sleep?"

"Have you?"

He felt his nerves begin to snap.

"Please, let's not play that scene again. Not now. I almost got picked up along with your brother."

He sat down at the table and sipped the coffee. He hadn't realized how shaken he was, and now he felt a little faint. Rosalie ran her warm hand over his forehead.

"You look awful," she said. "What happened?"

"Oh, nothing much. All in a day's work I guess. Just another murder. Right in the room below us. A whore who was having trouble with a john."

"And? Who was killed?"

"The john. And you'll never guess who did it."

Her face flushed and then drained of color, and he leaned over to take her hand.

"I'm sorry. I didn't mean to upset you. I shouldn't be playing guessing games. No, it wasn't Junior. It was his new bodyguard. Gold tooth."

She didn't respond.

"Remember, the tooth I showed you that time in the office."

She nodded, and the color began to surface in her face.

"He's working for Junior. Only now maybe I should call him scarface."

"How'd all that happen?"

"I didn't get a chance to find out." He brought his fist down on the table. "Damn, I didn't get a chance to find out a lot of things. Like if Junior is going to let me turn him in. I mean, we sort of agreed, but we didn't set the where and the when, and now he's underground again."

"He'll get in touch."

Seymour frowned.

"Yeah, I know. Like always, just when you least expect it, there he is. But we're about out of time."

"Does he know that?"

"Yes."

"Then we'll hear from him very soon. He's no fool."

Seymour relaxed a bit, and finished his coffee.

"You're probably right. But still I wish that creep could have restrained himself and not gotten himself killed." He leaned back in his chair and lit a cigarette. "Some things I just don't understand. All this bondage shit. The woman took a beating."

"Maybe it'll teach her a lesson." Her voice had an edge, and Seymour was puzzled.

"You think it's her fault."

"I'm not saying that. Just that she could learn something from it, but she'll probably be right back on the streets tonight. Anyway," she said after a moment, "I think I had Lois in mind when I said it. I don't know exactly why."

"We're both a little rocky," he said.

Seymour felt the bile begin to rise in his stomach and he got to his feet. His legs did not behave, and the room spun. He closed his eyes against the memory of the deep purple bruises on the woman and the slit neck of the john, and realized that he had not even stopped to check if the man were still alive. He got up again and staggered over to the sink. He tasted the sourness at the back of his throat as he leaned over, but he could only manage a dry hacking cough, and then he stumbled into the bedroom.

He lay in bed on his back, alternately staring at the shadows on the ceiling and closing his eyes. He lit a cigarette, and that helped a little. He began to feel a little calmer, and his stomach was no longer forcing choking gases up into his throat. Rosalie had not joined him. He had heard her straightening up in the kitchen, the water running in the sink, but then silence. He thought he heard the front door open and close, and he strained to hear voices or steps padding down the hall. His forehead was clammy with sweat, and he shut his eyes so that the room would stop spinning. He felt a soft hand stroke his face.

"I thought I'd better give you some time alone," Rosalie said.

Seymour reached for her and drew her into the bed.

"No," he said. "I want you here."

Rosalie heard the knocking first, and by the time Seymour opened his eyes she had slipped out of bed. He saw her slip on his old flannel robe and step quietly out of the room. He heard the door click open, and then after a moment, a woman's voice. He could not make out the words, but the sound of the door closing and the scraping of two chairs on the kitchen floor was clear. He fought back the acid taste in his mouth and the throbbing in his head and stumbled to the bathroom. His face in the mirror was gaunt, his eyes red-rimmed, and his stubble thick and gray. He splashed some water on his face until he felt sufficiently awake to find out what Lois wanted this time.

She and Rosalie were sitting at the kitchen table, both with their backs erect and rigid in their chairs. Cups of tea sat untouched before them sending thin strands of vapor into the chill air. It looked as though they had been holding this position for some time, as they sought an answer to a vexing problem. Seymour tried to break the mood.

"Good morning, ladies." He forced warmth and some lightness into his words. Lois looked up for a moment and then turned back to Rosalie who remained motionless.

"There's coffee on the stove," she said without turning around.

Seymour poured himself a cup and pulled the stepstool over to the tiny kitchen table he had had since his student days. He sat down and looked at the two women. Rosalie had his robe bunched tightly around her, and she held it closed with one hand. Her uncombed hair stood out and her eyes were fixed on Lois. Lois still had her coat on, an imitation fur, probably meant to look like a fox. It was open, almost sliding off her shoulders, and she was wearing a tight jersey pullover under it. Her long hair flowed down her back and her face was fully made up with heavy red strokes on her cheeks and thick blue on her lids. Seymour could just see her bare thigh over the edge of the table.

She smiled at Seymour with a flutter of her heavy lashes.

"I was just telling your hausfrau that I have a message from your client. And one from me."

Rosalie stood up.

"You'll excuse me," she said, "but I have to get dressed."
She leaned over to kiss Seymour and held her lips against
his. Seymour sat quietly on his perch, waiting. The water
pipes knocked loudly as Rosalie turned on the shower.

"Well," he asked finally. "What was that all about?"

"Don't ask me," Lois replied. "You'll have to find out from
her."

He imagined Rosalie in the steamy bathroom, the cracked
mirror over the sink dripping with mist, and he parted the
shower curtain. Rosalie, her eyes closed and her head turned
up to the hot water, soaped her breasts with her bare hands.
She smiled, her arms reaching for him through the moist
air, her body long and lean, just the hint of hair under her
arms but rich and thick between her legs.

Lois brought her spoon down in a measured stroke against
the rim of her cup. "All rise," she said.

Seymour did not respond.

She frowned.

"Isn't that what they say when court is in session?"

He nodded. "And are you the judge?"

She threw off her coat and thrust out her chest. She stood
up and raised one foot onto the chair. Her skirt rose to her hip.

"Do you want to enter a plea, counselor?"

He removed her foot, his hand brushing the inside of her
thigh. He sat across from her.

"It looks like you have your work clothes on," he said.

She laughed.

"Counselor, how could you think that, so early in the
morning."

"Maybe you're just stopping off on your way home, then,"
he snapped.

Her face froze for a moment.

"Maybe I am."

He thought a second, and then shrugged.

"I guess, at this point, that's your business," he said.

She threw her head back and laughed before fixing him with her bright eyes.

"At this point? It's always been my business." She paused. "You, of all people, should know that."

"What's this about a message. Or messages?"

"The first," she said, "is from Junior."

"When did you see him?"

"Last night."

"Where?"

"Look," she said, her voice cold. "Let's make this easy. I talk, you listen. Then if you have questions, ask them."

She took a sip of her tea and put the cup down with a clatter. Her hand was shaking.

"I saw Junior, my man, your friend and client, last night. At home. I heard his voice. From the baby's room. He was saying good-bye." She took another sip, but this time held the cup between her hand. "He said to tell you, Friday morning, ten o'clock. No reporters, or no show. At the courthouse. You be there and he'll find you."

"That's all?"

"From him, yes."

"And you?"

"Just this. You probably won't see me for a while. Don't call. I'll be keeping odd hours. And I don't want any involvement. It's bad for business." She bit off the last words.

"And the baby?"

"How caring of you to ask? But everything's taken care of." She walked to the door.

"Just one more thing," she said.

Seymour waited. She stood with her hand on the knob.

"Get him home to me," she said. "I need him."

"When you saw him last night, did he say anything about our meeting?"

"No, he wouldn't. He doesn't talk about that with me. Ever."

Seymour nodded.

"Why?" she asked.

He took his time.

"Well, I just thought he might have mentioned how we both almost got caught at the scene of a pretty messy murder."

He searched her face for a reaction. When she did not respond, he continued.

"We met in your old downtown office."

She lowered her eyes for a second, and took her hand off the doorknob as though she had realized that it was hot. He thought he detected a quiver at the corner of her mouth, but then her face went blank. He had seen such expressions on the faces of defendants who were either lying or concealing information. He pushed a little harder.

"It seems that one of your old associates had a problem with a client. A fatal problem."

"Who?" she whispered.

"She calls herself 'Kitten.' She's okay, I guess, just a little the worse for wear. The client is, I expect, at the morgue."

She took a deep breath, and the mask cracked into an angry snarl.

"Shit! Isn't it just our luck?"

Rage rose within him.

"Luck! Luck doesn't have anything to do with it. The only luck we had was getting our asses out of there before the cops showed up. I don't know who tipped them, or if they were just making a regular visit." He shook his head as the idea flashed. "Maybe they had an appointment for crissakes, I don't know. I wouldn't be surprised. But what I do know is that I am an officer of the court, and I ran like a goddamned criminal."

His anger died as suddenly as it had erupted. "Look," he said. "Why don't you just go on your way. I'll show up at the courthouse, and we'll take it one step at a time from there."

She started to reply when they heard steps on the stairs.

"Are you expecting company?" she asked.

He shook his head and half-smiled.

"No, but I can guess."

"So can I."

He turned toward Rosalie who stood in the doorway to the kitchen, her face glowing olive rich from the shadow, her black hair hanging damply to her shoulders. She was wearing a baggy sweatshirt and worn jeans.

"I'm sure," she said, "it's our friendly neighborhood detective. You two better sit down and figure out what you want to say to him while I answer the door and give him my best 'we're all such nice folks' librarian's smile." She moved toward the door just as the bell rang, but turned back to Lois. "Maybe you can keep your legs crossed and underneath the table while our guest is here." She tossed a newspaper toward her. "You can kind of spread this out in front of you."

Lois pushed the newspaper away from her with the tips of her fingers.

"I don't know what you think I've got to hide," she said, "but I never read that paper. Too grim. I want one with comics, horoscope, and advice to the lovesick, that's my favorite."

"I'm sure," Rosalie said. Her lips hardly moved, and then she turned to answer the door.

Seymour heard the door click open, but no voices. He turned to look and saw Rosalie gesturing toward the kitchen.

"You know, some days are just luckier than others," Detective Rosenberg said. "Here I hoped to find Mr. Constantino's attorney so that I could check on his client's whereabouts, when we might have the pleasure of a conversation, and what do you know, I luck out and get the whole family."

Lois nudged Seymour's ribs. "So this is the big, bad man," she whispered. "We go back a long way. I'll take care of him."

She motioned the detective into the kitchen.

"Reuben, howya' doin'? Come on in and take a load off. Seymour, is there more coffee for Reuben?"

Detective Rosenberg nodded to Lois, but his face remained impassive.

"It's been a long time," he said.

"Too long," Lois replied. Seymour studied her eyes. The pupils seem dilated and unfocused. He leaned across the table and took her hand.

"Maybe you should go freshen up. I'm sure the detective will excuse you. You do have that appointment uptown you were just telling me about."

She pulled her hand free.

"Sure, sure, but not before I have a chance to chat with Reuben. He was the first one to bust me, years ago, when he was in uniform. I'll never forget the look on his face when I was out the door almost before he was. After a while, we came to a kind of understanding. But look at him now, dressed like a banker or something."

"I've heard there've been some changes for you, too," the detective said. "I hear you've got a little baby at home, and that you've been off the streets. I hope that's the case."

"It was," Lois said.

"And still is?" Rosenberg asked.

"We do what we have to do," she answered, her eyes now narrowed and bright.

"I'm sorry to hear that."

Seymour half believed that the detective was genuinely concerned, but he mistrusted him. Whatever else might motivate him at the moment, he was O'Riley's man, and he wanted Junior any way he could get him. He turned to Rosenberg.

"What can we do for you? I'm sure there must be something extraordinary to bring you here."

"No, not so special. It's all part of my job, and I kind of

like being back in this neighborhood. I used to know it well."

"Well, detective," Seymour said in his crisp courtroom voice, "it's interesting to discover your roots, professional, or social . . ."

Rosenberg waved his hand in a gesture of dismissal.

"Professional," he said, "I was raised . . ."

"Wherever, whatever," Seymour cut him off. "Please don't think me rude, but I'd like to try to cooperate with you, and then go about my business."

"As you like, Mr. Lipp. But I think, maybe, your business is also mine. In any case, perhaps you can answer a couple of questions for me."

"About?"

"About a murder last night. A knifing in a room above a restaurant, The Sitar, off Avenue D. I think Mrs. Constantino here, knows the place."

Seymour glanced at Lois who was sitting with her elbows on the table, her hands cupping her chin. Her face was set in a look of bemused interest like that of one who is being told an anecdote involving people from faraway lands, wondering what possible connection she might have with the story. Her eyes were half closed, and she puffed slowly on a cigarette. When Rosenberg mentioned the restaurant and her name, she permitted a flicker of a smile to slide across her lips, but she did not say anything.

"I think I know the place," Seymour said.

"I thought you might," Rosenberg responded.

"I am partial to Indian food, and I'm sure I've wandered by it from time to time, though I've never tried it."

"And last night?"

"Excuse me?" Seymour wondered when the detective would shift gears.

"Last night, Mr. Lipp. Did you happen to be wandering in that neighborhood, in or near the restaurant, between, let's say, midnight and three a.m?"

"No, I can't say that I was. I believe we had pizza last night, at about six or seven." He looked to Rosalie and was pleased to see that she nodded and that her eyes were warm.

Detective Rosenberg straightened himself in his chair and shifted so that he faced Seymour directly.

"Then you wouldn't know anything about a john getting himself offed last night after he got a little too rough. We found him with his throat slit, nice neat job, from ear to ear."

Seymour calculated how much the detective could know. He saw the room again, the nude man's body on the floor, the bruised woman holding her clothes around her heaving body, but none of that provided a connection. And then he remembered that he wasn't sure that Pedro and Kitten had gotten away. He decided to gamble.

"Can't say as I do," he said.

The detective opened his notebook and held his pen poised above a page.

"Where were you last night, sir, just for the record?"

"What record is that?"

"My report, Mr. Lipp, the report of my investigation."

"Are you including me in your report of this murder?"

"Could you answer the question, Mr. Lipp? It's just a formality. You should understand that."

"I'm afraid you've lost me, detective. There must be a piece missing."

Rosenberg placed his open notebook on the table in front of him and laid his pen across the page.

"Oh, yes, of course, the piece. You see, Mr. Lipp, that room, behind the restaurant you say you know, is one of Mr. Constantino's old resting places. We've been doing some digging around, you know, trying to locate your client, and our information is that he has been known to burrow into that building. It's kind of like his corporate headquarters."

"And is that the piece?"

Rosenberg shook his head.

"Of course not, Mr. Lipp. That was just a lead that brought us there. The piece has to do with a credit card."

"Excuse me?" Seymour asked, but he already knew that he had been snared.

"To be precise, sir, your card. We found it on a young man we now have in custody, one Pedro Rivera. We picked him up in the neighborhood. Maybe you know him. Has a long scar on his cheek and a gold tooth. The hooker got away."

"Rivera," Seymour mused. "I don't think I know anybody by that name. In any case, I misplaced my wallet some time ago, and when I recovered it the cards were gone, along with a few dollars."

"Just asking," Rosenberg said, his hand on the door. "It seems Mr. Rivera is a business associate of Mr. Constantino. Strange how he should wind up with your American Express card. Almost like he was keeping it as a souvenir."

Seymour shrugged.

"If it were the gold card, maybe I could understand."

"Just a thought, Mr. Lipp. It seemed like a lead worth tracking down." He turned to Lois. "By the way, you wouldn't happen to know where Mr. Constantino was last night, would you?"

Lois smiled broadly.

"My husband was home last night, paying attention to our daughter."

"And now?"

Lois shrugged.

"I can't help you with that detective."

"But I can," Seymour said. "I have been in touch with Mr. Constantino, quite recently, and I can assure you that he will soon be available for questioning."

Detective Rosenberg frowned.

"You could have saved me a lot of trouble if you had told me that before. When will that be, counselor?"

"Soon."

"Can't you pin that down any better?"

"I'd like to help you, but that's the best I can do."

"You know we have a warrant."

"Yes."

"And that time is running out."

"Yes detective, we know all of that, and my client is prepared to cooperate fully. He's anxious to get this matter straightened out."

Rosenberg raised his eyebrows.

"You could have fooled me." He turned toward the door. "Has Mr. Rivera been charged?"

"No, not yet. He's got a Public Defender."

"I see," Seymour said. "I wasn't looking for business."

"I didn't think so," Rosenberg said. He opened the door, waved good-bye, and left.

"That's enough excitement for one day." Rosalie had resumed her place at the table, across from Lois who had not changed her position.

Seymour leaned over her to make sure he had Lois' attention. "He will show on Friday, won't he?"

"Sure," she answered. Her voice was flat, disinterested. "He's no fool. He's just playing the hand out." She got up slowly and stretched. "I'd like to say it's been fun, but I've got to be on my way."

"We'll keep in touch," Seymour said. He noticed Rosalie stiffen for a moment.

"I told you about that," Lois said. "I'm out."

"I wish it was that simple."

"It is for me." She turned to Rosalie. "Don't bother. I can find my own way out."

Rosalie nodded, but did not say anything. After Lois shut the door behind her, she started to clear the cups and saucers from the table. Seymour took her arm in his hand. She started to pull it away.

"What was all that about?" he asked.

She look at him, her eyes wide and hurt.

"Don't you know?"

"I'm not sure that I do."

She brushed a tear from her eye."

"I didn't know you could be so dense. If I have to explain it, it just makes it worse."

Seymour felt his patience snap.

"What 'it' are we talking about? The 'it' of Lois the hooker, the 'it' of Lois my one-time lover, that's a twisted and bizarre one, the 'it' of Lois the wife of your brother, or mother to his child, your niece, or Lois the addict?" He slammed his first on the table so that a cup rolled to the edge. He caught it before it fell. Rosalie's hand arrived a half second later and held his.

"All of them," she said quietly, "all of them." After a moment, she forced a smile. "But mostly the kinky one."

The building was as impressive as Seymour had imagined it to be, rising in stately lines from the avenue, its upper floors, beneath the exotic gargoyles, commanding a view of the park across the street. He walked toward the doorman who was looking at him without concern. Goode had insisted that they meet, had wanted to take him out to lunch or dinner. Seymour had pushed for a conference in his office, but Goode had declined saying something about not having the time to travel to Brooklyn. They both knew that they were maneuvering for a territorial edge, and reluctantly Seymour had conceded. Tomorrow he would be dealing with the police and Junior. Maybe the old man could be of some help, although Seymour still hadn't decided how far he was willing to walk the shady paths of Mr. Goode. For now, he hoped to discover the direction of those ways, to measure the distance against his own boundaries.

He ground out his cigarette on the sidewalk and raised a

disapproving stare from the doorman who leaned over to pick up the butt as though he were disposing of a dead rat. He dropped the cigarette into an ashtray by the door and turned to Seymour.

"Can I help you sir?"

"I have an appointment with Mr. Goode. My name's Lipp. He's expecting me."

The doorman's expression of scornful civility did not change. He punched in a code on the intercom, and after a few words that Seymour could not hear, he held the door open.

"Apartment 1223," he said. "The elevator is to your right."

He had not expected Goode to waste any time with amenities, but the old man did not even say hello. As soon as Seymour walked into the apartment, Goode was on him.

"You took your time getting here, Lipp. Look, I've just heard something awful." Goode looked and sounded heavy with his years in contrast to the buoyancy of their first meeting. "Now. Have you turned up anything on Gomez? When is your man going to be questioned?"

"Do you mind if I sit down for the Inquisition?" Seymour asked. They were standing in a hallway lined with original oil paintings, one of which Seymour thought was a Chagall, but he wasn't sure. Goode ushered him into the living room, which was dominated by a life-size wrought-iron sculpture of a figure that appeared to be a woman, half kneeling on one knee, arms crossed in front of her chest, as though in supplication. The room was plushly carpeted in ivory with several oriental rugs scattered about, seemingly at random. The tables were all chrome and glass and the upholstered furniture angular and uncomfortable looking. Seymour took a step toward the sofa, his eyes still drawn to the sculpture, but Goode continued steering him through the room.

"Nobody ever sits in here," he said. "It's my wife's project.

When she's here. I sent her to Paris until this thing blows over." He followed Seymour's eyes.

"Emily did that," he said. "Years ago. Beatrice changes everything else in the room, but that remains. Always."

They passed through a door into a smaller room, an office cluttered with a huge wooden desk, papers strewn across its surface, bookshelves sagging beneath ledgers. A calendar supplied by a furrier's organization occupied the only open wall space. The illustration for the month was a bosomy brunette wearing only a mink stole. Goode sat behind his desk, and motioned for Seymour to sit on an overstuffed and ancient loveseat against the wall across from the desk.

"Lipp," Goode said, leaning his jowled face toward Seymour, "I'm sure Gomez is our man."

"Because you think he used to be one Eduardo Rodriguez."

Goode started.

"I knew I shouldn't underestimate you."

"My assistant dug up that bit."

"Well, whatever," Goode rose and paced the room, his thick body animated by his anger. "It's clear, isn't it? The son-of-a-bitch waits all these years. To get back at me, would you believe it, to pay me back, for what he did!"

"We're going a little fast," Seymour began, but Goode waved his hand impatiently.

"Fast? How did he slip through, that's the question. A simple name change. Shit, I had the best people on it."

"Then, they blew it," Seymour said.

"No! Not them me, and now twice. But no more. He's mine, if I do nothing else."

"If all of this checks out, you'll have him."

"If? What if? And your man is free."

"The 'if' is evidence, like maybe physical evidence, something more than a crazy story about a man waiting fifteen or twenty years for revenge."

Goode considered.

"Not so crazy. Not if you know the man. Like I do."

"I intend to find out," Seymour said.

"For your sake," Goode replied, "I hope you find out the right thing."

"Didn't you make that mistake once before?"

Goode looked taken aback for a moment.

"No, I don't think so. I was right then, as I am now."

"Maybe. But a day or so ago, you were sure you had the right scum in your sights. Remember?"

"Scum is scum, that doesn't change." He settled deeper into his chair, his shoulders weighed down in exhaustion, but he stirred himself.

"I'll say this kindly, don't get in my way. I mean to punish the bastard. With or without your cooperation."

Seymour stood.

"I'm really tired of threats. Maybe Gomez is our man. But I can tell you that Junior will turn himself in tomorrow for questioning. I do not know if the police will hold him or if he will be formally charged. Anyway, I will try to run down Gomez."

"And I can tell you that I know tomorrow morning's papers are going to have Mr. Constantino's face all over the front page."

"O'Riley wouldn't do that."

"Wouldn't he? I think you know better than that."

"We had an arrangement," Seymour began, but then he caught himself. "We both know what that means."

Goode waved his hand deprecatingly.

"Tomorrow is not so much. You'll go in, answer a few questions. Maybe they'll hold your man. Maybe not. The newspapers will play it big, but it's coming on the weekend, so not too bad. Anyway I have reason to believe O'Riley might lose the front page to the stock market. But, here's the important thing, you just leave Gomez to me. Soon enough, I'll hand him to them."

"I'm not committing myself to anything," Seymour said as he turned to go. "Tomorrow, I'll be protecting Junior."

"That's right, you do that," Goode said. He had taken Seymour by the arm again, and they walked back through the living room. "You just worry about your friend."

Seymour folded the morning newspaper under his arm and entered the stationhouse. He scanned the large room he found himself in. Detectives sat at desks, some questioning suspects, others filling out reports. Two uniformed officers came in with a young black man, hands handcuffed behind his back, between them. As they passed Seymour, the young man stopped walking for a moment. His eyes flashed hatred and anger. One of the officers squeezed his arm hard and pushed him forward to the sergeant's desk. The other officer dropped a packet on the desk.

"Martin Davis. He was holding," the officer said.

"Like shit I was," the young man mumbled.

A detective strolled over and smiled at Davis. Then he turned to the sergeant. He picked up the packet, opened it, passed it under his nose, and then tasted the powder from the tip of his index finger.

"Book him," he said. He turned to the young man. "Where'd you get such good shit?"

Davis struggled to twist himself free and kicked out at the detective. The detective stepped back as though avoiding being splashed by a car riding through a puddle.

"Now, Martin, why don't you just behave yourself. You've been through all this before. It always comes out the same way."

The detective straightened his suit jacket, and his eyes landed on Seymour.

"Can I help you, sir?" he asked.

"If you don't mind me hanging around for a few minutes

until my client shows up," Seymour said, "I'll have all the help I need."

The detective raised his eyebrows. He was a burly man with a beefy and pocked face. He chewed a toothpick. He walked over to the desk sergeant and came back with a visitor's pass that he stuffed in Seymour's breast pocket.

"Mind, no I don't mind. Make yourself comfortable. I'm Detective Rosario."

"Seymour Lipp."

"Well, Mr. Lipp, can I ask who you are waiting for?" Seymour smiled.

"You know you can ask, but until he shows up, I guess there's not much point in my answering."

The detective narrowed his eyes and bit down on his toothpick.

"No, I guess not," he said. "Here, I got some business to take care of back there." He motioned down the hall to the interrogation rooms. "You can wait at my desk for a while."

Seymour pressed the newspaper tighter against his side and walked to the cluttered desk with Rosario's nameplate on it.

"Thanks," he said. "It shouldn't be long."

"Take your time," Rosario said. "I'll be tied up for a while. Oh, and help yourself to a cup of coffee if you want."

Seymour fixed himself some coffee and sat at Rosario's desk, the newspaper spread out before him. Goode had been half right. The headlines blared doom about the market collapsing, but Junior appeared in the lower left corner in a sketch that was a fair likeness. He wondered why O'Riley hadn't provided a mug shot. Probably, he thought, because the prosecutor believed an artist's rendering of a psychopath would have more kick than the subdued face of a man once in custody. He skimmed over the copy and saw that it was more innocuous than the picture, only name and occupation and the fact that Junior was wanted for questioning and might provide a break in this terrible case. Seymour saw the restraint of the copy as a lid sitting uneasily over the cauldron of O'Riley's need to answer his opponent's criticism of him, which was featured in an adjoining story. He also had the uneasy feeling that everyone in the stationhouse knew why he was there. He lit a cigarette and blew the smoke into the stale air, realizing after a moment that he wanted the smoke to screen him from searching eyes.

He knew that he shouldn't be sitting at Rosario's desk, expecting Junior to materialize. It was a few minutes after ten o'clock. Maybe Junior was already in the stationhouse, but how was he supposed to find him? Absentmindedly, he stared down the hallway in the direction Rosario had taken. He heard a workman humming while he replaced a bulb in the fluorescent ceiling fixture. He jumped, but Junior put his finger to his lips and motioned toward the door. Seymour turned just in time to see Detective Rosenberg push through the door ahead of two officers who had a small, sullen figure of a man between them. The man was staring at the floor as he walked, so Seymour could not be sure at first, but then the man raised his eyes to take in the room. He curled his lips in a sneering smile, his gold front tooth clearly visible. Rosenberg led him to the sergeant's desk and said something that Seymour could not hear. He turned toward Seymour and waved, and Seymour nodded a greeting. The officers led Pedro away, and Rosenberg strolled over to Seymour.

"Know him?" Rosenberg asked.

Seymour thought for a moment.

"Tell you the truth, he looks like a thousand street punks I've run across."

"Well, this one is special."

"Anything besides his gold tooth?"

Rosenberg smiled.

"Oh, yes." He paused. "He's the one I was telling you about in connection with the john killing, the one who somehow came into possession of your credit card."

"Did he do it?"

Rosenberg shrugged.

"I'm just the catcher, you know. Other people decide if my fish is legal size. If not, they get tossed back to swim in their slime." Rosenberg grinned. "But I don't have to tell you about that counselor, do I?"

"Well," Seymour said slowly, "I don't think I'd have used the same language, but we both know how the system works."

The grin disappeared from Rosenberg's face, replaced by his cynical and weary professional mask.

"Or doesn't," he said simply. "Let me know when your man turns up. I'll be in Room 4, down the hall. He'll probably know the way."

Seymour followed Rosenberg's back with his eyes until he passed the ladder on which Junior had been standing. It was empty, and the detective stopped to glance around the hallway before continuing on his way. He disappeared into an interrogation room. Seconds later, Junior emerged from the men's room and motioned to Seymour. He was wearing jeans and a parka.

"Let's do it," he said.

"Just a minute," Seymour protested, and placed his hand on Junior's arm. "First, I thought Halloween was a couple of weeks ago. Why the costume?"

Junior shrugged.

"It's just my way, man. You should know that."

"Second. They've brought Pedro in for questioning."

Junior flashed a smile.

"They're just dancin'. They don't have nothin'."

"Maybe yes, maybe no. But what happens if Pedro decides it would be in his interest to implicate you."

Junior frowned.

"In the first case, no way. Pedro ain't gonna turn. He's

been through this mill before, and he knows that he'll be ground meat. And, besides, he don't have no use for these officers of the law." Junior paused, and then drew Seymour closer to him so that he could whisper into his ear.

"One of them bastards did his sister when he was bringin' her in for liftin' a couple of pieces of shit jewelry. She was thirteen. Pedro lives to find out which one it was. When he does, there'll be one less cop. In the meantime, he ain't gonna tell them nothin'. You can count on it."

"I guess we'll have to." Seymour backed away so that he could look directly into Junior's face. "Are you ready. Do you know what you're going to say. We should have talked this out."

"Be cool, man. It's your job to make sure that I don't have to say much of anything, and what I do have to answer, well, for that I'll figure somethin' out."

"Great," Seymour said. "Just great."

They sat around a small table, Junior next to Seymour, Rosenberg and another detective across from them. Vesta, the second detective, looked like a character from an old black-and-white gangster movie, Seymour thought, in which suspects were interrogated with a rubber hose in places that didn't leave marks. He was short and squat, his rounded jaw resting on his chest and his belly pushing against his shirt buttons that seemed ready, at any moment, to fly off. He chewed gum and said little.

"As I've said," Seymour repeated, his eyes on Rosenberg, "my client would like to cooperate fully and expeditiously. He will do his best to answer your questions."

Vesta blew a large bubble and popped it. Seymour stared at him, and he smiled back.

"That's all well and good, Mr. Lipp," Detective Rosenberg said, "but you can understand that Mr. Constantino's refusal to present himself for questioning before this point has raised some questions about his sincerity in our minds. We are naturally suspicious."

"That's your job," Seymour replied. "And it is mine to be certain that those suspicions are not misplaced. Mr. Constantino agreed to come in as soon as I was able to contact him." Seymour improvised. "He left his job suddenly, and I might add temporarily, to attend to some personal matters, and it was only recently that I had the chance to speak to him." He paused. "When I did, and learned that you had your 'suspicions,' he asked me to arrange this meeting so we could straighten this matter out."

Detective Vesta tossed a paper bag on the table and turned it over so that the gray workman's clothes spilled out.

"What was the idea?" he asked.

Junior smiled and leaned across the table to straighten the clothes.

"Careful, I only rented these for the hour, and I promised to return them in good shape."

Vesta brought his large fist down on the table, an inch or so from Junior's hand.

"Right," he said. "But maybe you won't have the chance to bring them back. Maybe you'll be wearing something very much like them, only with a number on it."

Rosenberg frowned at Vesta, and the large man moved back from the table. Seymour took his newspaper and slapped it on the table next to the clothes.

"I could ask," he said, "about the meaning of this. We do not appreciate being tried in the newspapers before any formal charges have been offered."

"Let's call us even on the fun and games for now," Rosenberg said smoothly. "You know that isn't my style, and not my idea."

"I'm not sure even is the right word," Seymour answered. "But let's get down to business."

"Fine," Rosenberg said. He took out his notebook and

flipped through the pages. "Mr. Constantino, did you have a relationship with Emily Levine?"

Junior smiled.

"Sure. She asked me if I could get her some coke, and I said I didn't do that business anymore. I had promised Mr. O'Riley that I wouldn't, and I'm a man of my word."

Rosenberg did not look up from his notebook as he continued.

"Isn't it true that you slept with her?"

Junior turned to Seymour, who saw Rosenberg's brows furrow, and he leaned across to Junior.

"You don't have to admit anything," he whispered, "but let's give them this one, straight, no jokes. They've got a half a dozen witnesses who'll swear that you were making it with Emily in every corner of that building."

Junior drew back from Seymour and his eyes turned serious.

"My counselor here is advising me that I haven't been takin' this line of questions serious enough. So here's the straight answer. Yes. Mrs. Levine came after me. For sex. And we were together a few times, but that all stopped months ago."

"Why's that?" Vesta asked from his corner in the room.

Junior looked steadily at him.

"One of us got bored."

"Which?" Vesta asked.

"Guess," Junior said.

Seymour was watching Rosenberg closely, and he saw the detective's mouth tighten.

"My client admits having a relationship with the victim. Can we move on?"

"Sure," Rosenberg said. "Was she carrying your baby?" His voice remained calm, almost bored.

Junior began to respond, but Seymour nudged him hard. "Let me earn my money," he said, and then he turned to the detective. "We have no knowledge of Mrs. Levine's condition before she was murdered."

Rosenberg moved his pencil over the page and nodded.

"Do you carry a switchblade knife? Perhaps for protection?" Rosenberg permitted himself a half smile, but his voice was as bland as though he were reading items on a grocery list.

"That would be a violation of our custodial order," Seymour said.

Rosenberg looked up at Seymour.

"Of course, it would." He fixed his eyes on Junior. "Could you answer the question please?"

Junior paused, and then said, "No."

"Where were you on the night of the murder, November 2nd?"

Junior did not hesitate.

"Home, watching wrestling. With my wife. We had a bet on."

"Who won?" Rosenberg asked.

"She did," Junior replied.

"The match?"

"I think it was the Hulk."

"Can anybody else confirm your whereabouts for that evening and night."

"I don't know," Junior replied.

"Do you know anything about a hooker named Tanya, also known, among other aliases, as Kitten?"

"I used to know a lot of hookers."

"Even married one, so's I hear." Vesta chuckled, an ugly leer on his face. Junior leaped to his feet, but both Rosenberg and Seymour restrained him. After a moment, he relaxed, but his eyes remained intense. Rosenberg scowled at Vesta. "Just trying to lighten things up," the large detective said.

"That will about do it." Rosenberg folded his notebook and turned to Vesta. "Book him," he said. "The charges are suspicion of aggravated assault, rape, and second-degree murder."

Vesta eased himself out of the room. He returned in a matter of seconds with two uniforms. They must have been waiting by the door, Seymour thought. Junior stood up, his face a mask of grinning indifference. He held out his hands to be cuffed.

"That won't be necessary," Rosenberg said.

"Be seeing you around," Vesta said. "In about ten to twenty."

Junior brought his hand down over his fly.

"That's the only thing you'll be seein'." Each officer grabbed one of his arms and escorted him out of the room.

Rosenberg stood up and stretched.

"Mr. Lipp," he said, "your client is not helping himself with this behavior, even recognizing some provocation."

"I'm only his lawyer," Seymour said, and followed Junior and the officers out of the door.

It was snowing lightly, the kind of early snow in the city that looks like a blizzard when magnified by the glare of streetlights but that dissipates to a thin white dust on the ground. Seymour was driving Rosalie's little Toyota, and he kept it in second gear as he peered through the windshield looking for his turnoff. The snow softened the crunch of the tires and the slap of the windshield wipers. Even the thunderous crashing of the waves was more like the beat of a muffled drum.

He fumbled for a cigarette and groped for the lighter. He looked down and found it next to the ashtray. When he raised his eyes, he saw somebody on a bike wobbling in the middle of the road just ahead of him. He took his foot off the gas, and the car slowed to just about the same speed as the biker. His car closed the distance gradually, and as he neared he studied the shape huddled over the handlebars.

He saw a shock of gray hair protruding from beneath a wool cap, and a brightly colored scarf flapped behind the elderly man. Two wire baskets mounted over the rear wheel carried paper bags of groceries, and the bike seemed ready at any moment to fall to one side or the other.

Seymour was sure that Schotelheim was the rider. He thought of beeping his horn to catch the old man's attention, but he decided instead to follow at a safe distance. The rider turned down a block, and Seymour began to steer the car after him. He caught a glimpse of the street sign and let the car slide to a gradual stop. For a while he watched the bike recede into the snow, and then he turned back onto the main street.

When he found the house, several blocks farther up the road, he saw that the surface of the snow around it showed no tracks of man or vehicle. He parked the car and approached the house, knowing before he got close enough to see that the old man would not be there. The house was boarded up, and a realtor's sign had been driven into the ground near the front door. Seymour brushed the snow from his face, and walked slowly around the house to the back. At least the surf did not disappoint him. It thundered hard against the shore, and he imagined the angry black curls of the ocean beneath the blowing flakes.

He felt a hand on his shoulder, and he turned around. An old woman, a coarse shawl wrapped around her head and face peered back at him.

"He's gone," she said, "put the house up for sale a couple of weeks ago. I don't know where he went."

"I'm an old friend," Seymour said.

The woman pulled the shawl from her eyes so that she could get a better look at him.

"I used to work for him, some time ago, and since then I've tried to keep in touch."

"What's your name?" she asked.

Seymour told her.

"He left a message for you. He said to tell you that he was sorry."

"That's all?"

The old woman nodded sadly and shuffled off in the dark.

Seymour made his way back to the car, got in, and rolled his window down. He sat for a long time listening to the surf, muted by the thick curtain of snow, and he imagined the vivid white crests of the waves turning in on themselves and burrowing into the soft belly of the cold, black water.

Seven

ON THE OTHER SIDE of the glass, Junior picked up the phone. Seymour waited, holding his own receiver to his ear, but all he heard was a loud crackling. Junior motioned for them to try again, and when they each picked up their receivers this time, the line was clear.

"You have to wonder," Seymour said, "how they can screw up a three-foot connection."

Junior's face broke into a laugh.

"Three feet, my ass," he said into the phone. "This line has to go all the way to the recording booth and back. We probably caught some dude comin' back from his coffee break." He tapped his mouthpiece against the glass and then brought it back to his ear. "Ready when you-all are," he drawled.

Junior smiled again, and Seymour felt his own mouth widen for a moment. He checked himself and coughed into the phone.

"Can I remind you that in a couple of days we have to appear for presentment and see what we can do about bail so that we can get you out of here. So maybe we should get down to business."

"Whatever you say, counselor. That's what I'm paying you such big bucks for."

"You couldn't pay me enough to take this case," Seymour snapped.

"Good thing, too," Junior said smoothly, "as you know." He knit his brows. "I've been meanin' to ask you that, you know."

"Why I'm doing this?"

Junior nodded, and Seymour sought an answer. Finally, he shrugged.

"I don't think I can tell you why. I wish I could, as much for me as you."

Junior grinned.

"In my crowd, you'd be considered an ass."

"Maybe," Seymour said, "that is why you're on that side of the glass."

Junior's eyes blazed.

"Maybe it is, but I don't think so any more than you do."

Seymour waved his hand to the side.

"Let's not argue that, for gods sake, we don't need a philosophical or psychological discussion right now."

"Right you are, as usual. Just so we understand each other. Anyway, like you said, down to business. I won't need bail."

Seymour shook the phone as if by doing so the words would come right.

"How's that?" he asked.

Junior's face was perfectly serious.

"It's not gonna get that far. Listen closely. I've been pickin' up some things while I'm in here, things about Gomez, that I'd like to check out. So why don't you just relax, and try not to lose your self-respect, on my account."

"And since I'll be relaxing, waiting for a rabbit to be pulled out of the hat, what should I be doing with my time?"

"Keepin' out of the way, man." His eyes darkened and his lips tensed. "And lookin' after Lois. You are keepin' an eye on her, like you promised?"

The lie died in Seymour's mind before he could utter it.

"I'm afraid that she's not making that very easy."

"Yeah, I guess so. I know she's gonna do what she's gonna do. It's just the damned baby." He paused, as though reflecting. "The hell with her. It's the baby. Look, just do what you can, alright."

"I've already said that I would."

"Okay. Good." He closed his eyes, apparently lost in thought.

"Are you sure about this Gomez thing?"

"Like I said, I've been hearin' things, but inside you hear a lot of shit, so I gotta check it out. But if the word is righteous, he's gonna fall."

Seymour took a deep breath.

"Are you sure of this?"

Junior nodded.

Seymour's memory flashed to Emily Levine's abused body, the blood congealing on her white flesh, and he stared at the hard lines of Junior's face.

"Why the 'fall'?" he asked. "Didn't you tell me that you were sure he did it? Remember?"

Junior shrugged.

"Sometimes I can be right, too. You don't have a lock on that."

"I want," Seymour said slowly, putting his full weight on each word as though by doing so he could make Junior feel his intention, "to be right about you."

Junior's gaze had narrowed to the space between them as Seymour spoke. He squeezed his receiver until the veins on his neck seemed to throb. His face was black with constrained fury.

"The only thing you have to want," Junior said through clenched teeth, "is for me to walk. And that means keepin' out of the way." His face relaxed into a bright smile. "That's the easy way, and the right way. A smart man knows when he's overmatched."

"You're beginning to sound like Mr. Goode."

Junior leaned back in his chair, began to reply, and then looked over his shoulder at the guard who was indicating time was up. Seymour followed his eyes, and then shuffled his papers together.

"There is one more thing." He considered how to make the request, but a guard was walking toward him. "Rosalie," he said simply, "wants to see you."

Junior did not hesitate.

"No way. Not until I'm out and this mess is over."

Seymour rode with the anger.

"I don't have her on a leash, you know."

"Maybe you'd better get one," Junior snapped. "But keep her away from me."

"Too, late. She's coming in right behind me," he said and got up to leave.

"I hope she ain't wired," Junior shouted at him.

"Maybe I shouldn't have talked to him," Rosalie said. She and Seymour were waiting for the elevator in the visitor's area. Her voice quivered. Seymour reached for her hand, but she pulled it away.

"No," she snapped. "I don't need any more of that." She leaned against the call button for the elevator. Seymour saw her shoulders heave, and when she turned to face him again, she was wiping the damp spots by her eyes with the tips of her fingers.

"I'm sorry," she whispered, "but that's how he treated me. Like the little, kid sister. We're all each of us has, really, but in his eyes I'm still the little girl, and he sees it as his job to make sure that I don't fall, and to pick me up, and make nice, nice, right away if I should. I just can't stand it."

Seymour moved his head back as though to remove himself from the circle of her anger. But he had to ask the question.

"Did he say anything," he sought for the right words, "about his involvement?"

"You mean did he say whether he did it?" Her voice cut him. "Why are you playing lawyer with me? Now of all times." She started to move away, but he held her arm.

"Okay," he said. "But I have to know."

She searched his eyes.

"Don't you think I have to, as well, and even more so?"

He nodded.

"He said that he didn't do it."

"Do you believe him?"

She averted her eyes for a moment, and when she again faced him, the pain seemed visibly etched on her face.

"Please, don't push me on this. He's my brother. I want to believe him. But I can only tell you what he said." She took a deep breath. "And he did say one more thing, something he thought you would understand."

Seymour leaned closer to her so that his face almost brushed against hers, but she moved away.

"He said that the Gomez business was going 'to go down real soon, but maybe with a bang.' Those were his words exactly. And 'you should remember the easy road.' "

"That's a warning."

"Yes. And?"

"Am I going to heed it? Where your brother is concerned I have a real problem doing that."

"I know," she said, her voice soft with resignation. "But I think you should." She took him by the arms. "I can't ask you to explain why you must be so damned stubborn. But know that I'll be with you every step of the way."

Several of the streetlights along the walkways in Gomez's project were out. As Seymour made his way through the shadows, he saw that the lamps had been smashed and that pieces of glass littered the ground around the stanchions. He narrowed his eyes and stood still for several minutes, but he saw nothing, no movement, no people, and he realized that that was the problem. Something was wrong. Even on a cold winter's night such as this, he had expected to find teenagers hanging out, and perhaps an adult or two returning home. Somebody. But he saw only shadows shifting like black skeletons suspended on invisible wires and stirred by the breeze into grotesque motions. At least, he thought, he had been able to convince Rosalie, over strenuous, objections, to look in on Lois, if not for Lois' sake, then for her niece and for her brother. He wasn't exactly sure why, maybe something in her manner after she spoke with Junior, but he wanted to do this one alone.

After several wrong turns, he stumbled on the building and pushed the door open. The lobby light was on, but the elevator didn't respond when he pushed the button. He found the stairs and started climbing them. His foot brushed against something soft and he jumped back. He didn't move for a few seconds. His fingers slid on a thick, cold liquid. He brought his head closer and saw that it was a puddle of some indistinguishable Chinese food next to an overturned container he had stepped on. He kicked the container to the side and started up the steps again.

Nobody answered his knock at the apartment door. He placed his ear against the door, but although he expected to hear the sound from the television, all was quiet. He stooped down to peer under the door, and the apartment inside appeared to be dark. He tried knocking again, waited, and then turned back to the stairway. He sat down on the landing, so that his body was hidden from the apartment door by the corner of the wall. After a few minutes he peered around the corner, and thought he saw the door move, just a little, and he pulled his head back. He heard nothing, and so he got up and walked to the door. Again, no one answered his knock. He returned to the landing and waited. Except for an occasional snatch of conversation drifting out from behind the other doors, the whole floor was quiet.

He trotted down the stairs, and just as he reached the first floor landing he heard a sharp crack and then a muffled thud that seemed to come from the basement. He hesitated for a moment, but remembering the figure he had seen crouching there, he decided to chance it.

The door to the basement was locked, and he banged his fist against it in frustration. As if in answer, the knob turned, and he pushed the door ajar. He sensed somebody on the other side, and so he hurled himself through the opening. He spun just in time to see a baseball bat crash against the floor. In the dim light he could see that the man holding the bat was Eddie Gomez. A few feet away, a large man lay crumpled in a heap.

Eddie lifted the bat up over his head and stared at Seymour.

"I thought you wanted to talk to me," Seymour said, as he raised his arm in front of his face.

Eddie stood motionless for a moment, his eyes staring hard at Seymour as though trying to remember, and then he eased the bat down. He leaned on it, much as he did his broom, and he cocked his head in his familiar gesture and cackled.

"Esmeralda, she call you, no?" He glanced at the man on the floor. "But then how do I know that you are not with him?"

"I'm not, and who the hell is that anyway?" Seymour kept his eyes on the bat.

Gomez shrugged.

"Just somebody," he said.

Seymour edged toward the man, and knelt down next to him.

"Do you mind?" he asked.

Eddie grinned.

"Sure, go ahead. He ain't gonna get up and go nowhere."

The man was lying face down, one arm twisted underneath him. He did not move while Seymour shoved him off the floor enough to pull out his wallet from his inside suit pocket, but Seymour did hear his slow breathing.

"I no kill him," Eddie offered. "I hit him here." He motioned toward the back of his neck. "And not so hard."

Seymour found an ugly red bruise just above the collar line of the man.

"He wanna get up in a while," Eddie said, "but we be gone by then."

Seymour flipped through the billfold that contained a thick wad of hundreds, but nothing else, no credit cards or papers.

"You don't find nothin' there," Eddie said.

"Did you take it?"

"Take what? What do I want to take from him?" Eddie spat and the thick globule landed at the man's feet.

"The badge," Seymour said.

"You crazy? That man, he want old Eddie real bad. No fuckin' badge."

Seymour understood. Of course, O'Riley wouldn't come after Gomez. Not now. Maybe never, if he still thought he could nail Junior.

"Do you think this guy's got any friends in the neighborhood?" he asked.

Eddie shrugged.

"Sure. Lots of friends. Don't matter. If they find me, I get them, one at a time, like him." He lifted the bat and brought it down in a sharp, violent arc. "One at a time. As many as he send. Maybe," he grinned, "the son-of-a-bitch come himself."

"You'd like that."

Eddie's eyes turned cold.

"Him, yeah, him I kill." He wagged the bat in front of him

like a hitter approaching the plate. "Baseball, it's the American game, no?"

Seymour wondered how long Gomez's fuse was, and decided that the direct approach was best.

"Like you killed his daughter?"

Seymour tensed, but Eddie only brought his hands to his face and rubbed his eyes.

"No, you got that wrong." His eyes narrowed. "Why do you think I have Esmeralda call you? To confess? What the hell I wanna do that for? When I didn't do nothin'."

"So? What's the deal?"

Eddie cocked his head and spat. Seymour now recognized the mannerism, as just that, a kind of screen dropped down in front of the man.

"No deal," Gomez said. "I didn't do nothin', like I said, but I saw plenty." He righted his head on his neck, and his eyes appeared bright and clear. "And what I saw was your friend, with his belt around her neck, and she had her eyes closed, and then she try to jump off him, but he just hold that belt real good."

"She was on top of him?"

Gomez stared at him.

"You never fuck that way?" he asked. "Esmeralda, she too fat for that."

Seymour nodded, but Gomez seemed to have lost his concentration. He swung the bat in lazy circles, inches above the floor. After a few moments, his eyes found Seymour again.

"Oh, you want all of it. Which I saw, all of it."

"What were you doing there?"

"That too, I tell you that." He crouched as though he had seen an insect on the floor. "You smart guy. You know I didn't just wind up in that building. I planned it. For a long time. I look at all the ads in the paper, and see the one about the new showroom, so I tell my parole officer, and he set it up for me. So I could be near her, watch her."

Seymour pushed, harder this time.

"Like you did, when she was a cute little thing, when you couldn't keep your hands off her?"

This time Eddie reacted in a leap toward Seymour that brought them both crashing down on the hard cement floor. Seymour shoved against Eddie's chest and squirmed free long enough to grab one end of the bat. Eddie slumped against the wall.

"I never touched her. I used to show her things in the garden. That's all. She get in trouble and say those things, but she lied." He drew in a deep breath. "I just wanted to ask her."

"Why she lied?" Eddie nodded. "That's all?"

"Maybe not, maybe something else," Gomez said. "But I didn't get no chance. I used to watch her with him. How he give her the stuff, and then they do it. But this time, she only wanted the stuff. Said she didn't need him for nothin' else. Said," he paused, "she got somebody new in mind." He leaned toward Seymour so that his face was inches away. "She tell him, she want you next."

Seymour got up with the bat in his hand and tossed it into the shadows. He heard it crack against the wall.

"You almost had me believing you," he said. "But you've left out a few things. Like how your arm got scratched up."

"I said there may be something else. I tried to talk to her. That night. But she was strung out. Waitin'. She needed it." He stood up, his eyes focused on the corner where Seymour had thrown the bat. "I put my hand on her shoulder, just so she wouldn't walk away, and she clawed me, and I tried to hold her harder, and then I heard him comin', so I let her go." He stopped for a moment.

"Later I find the body. I think about cutting it up and tossin' it in the incinerator. But I don't have no saw. So I call the cops and disappear," he said, and then he was gone into the darkness.

Seymour opened the outside door just enough to let his body through and then headed for a walkway about a hundred feet away that was still lit. When he was almost there, a shadow appeared and took human form. It circled behind him, and as he turned toward the movement something hard struck his ankles and he felt himself falling. He tried to catch himself, but a fist drove into his face. After the first kick, he hardly felt the thuds against his ribcage.

"Looks like somebody was trying to tell you something." Detective Rosenberg leaned over him and offered a handkerchief. Seymour was sitting, braced against the back of a bench. He could see the detective's car, it's red light flashing in the darkness. He took the handkerchief and dabbed at the blood flowing from the corner of his mouth. He tried a smile, but his lips were too swollen.

"I guess so," he managed to say. "And what do you think he wanted me to know?"

Rosenberg shrugged.

"Did he take anything?"

Seymour ran his hands through his pockets and then shook his head.

"I didn't think so," Rosenberg said. "It didn't look like that kind of business."

Seymour stood up and fought back the dizziness. His ribs throbbed.

"Maybe I should call an ambulance," Rosenberg said. "Don't worry about reporting this, or anything like that, I can take care of that."

Seymour tried to stop his head from spinning.

"Just tell me one thing," he said. "How'd you get here so fast?"

Rosenberg smiled.

"Let's just say I was in the neighborhood. Maybe looking for the same guy you were."

"Well, if you find him, you'd better be prepared to duck. There's a guy lying there in the basement, who didn't."

The detective frowned.

"Maybe I'm getting a step too slow."

"Or maybe Goode is just that much faster."

"It doesn't matter. I'll take you home. You got a big day coming up. The preliminary report on the physical evidence should be on O'Riley's desk in the morning."

Seymour waited for the alarm clock to ring. Rosalie was sleeping lightly next to him. Every once in a while, she would open her eyes and ask how he was. He would force a grim smile through his swollen lips and close his eyes and pretend to sleep.

Every breath jolted his ribcage. He timed these reminders of pointed leather crashing against his flesh so that their predictability became almost soothing, but his mind jumped from one half-formed idea to another. He stared hard at the ceiling, dimly lit by the glow from his clock until he could find the thin crack and follow it back to the corner where it disappeared in a spider's web. He stared until his eyes hurt, and then he closed them.

He leaned over, turned the alarm off and tried to slide out of bed. He grunted as he lifted his body up. Rosalie stirred and opened her eyes.

"What do you think you're doing?" she asked.

"Couldn't sleep, so I thought I might as well do something useful, like fix some breakfast."

"You could have asked me, you know."

He took a deep breath before trying to respond and doubled over. He felt like a truck had just rolled over his chest, and he fought to catch his breath.

"What you should do," she said, "is go to the hospital and get x-rayed. You've probably got two or three broken ribs."

For reasons he could not explain himself, he found her concern irksome.

"We'll make breakfast together," he said, "and then you'll try to check on Lois again, at least see if you can locate the kid. And I'll take the train in to O'Riley's office."

"If I didn't think it would hurt you too much, I'd sit on you so you couldn't go anywhere today."

He felt his annoyance dissipate, and he pretended to be considering her suggestion.

"Maybe we can try that tonight," he said.

"Lipp, why don't you do yourself a favor and let me send you to a hospital." O'Riley offered his wolf smile, full fanged. "Of course, I'm terribly sorry for what happened to you, but you can't expect me to know anything about it."

Seymour straightened himself in the plush chair, wishing that it offered more support for his back, and leaned his arms on O'Riley's polished desk.

"I don't know what I expect," he said slowly. "I was hoping for some simple, straight-up truth. Maybe I came to the wrong place."

O'Riley chuckled. He was unflappable. Seymour had to give him that. He would be very difficult in court, Seymour thought. The prosecutor seemed to be right with him.

"You know," he said, "I was also wondering what it would be like facing you. I rather like the idea."

"What makes you think that was on my mind?"

"The look on your face. I've seen it before." O'Riley closed his eyes in self-satisfaction for a moment. "Many times."

"Gas," Seymour said.

O'Riley focused on him.

"I beg your pardon," he said.

"The look you were just meditating on," Seymour said slowly, "it was gas."

"I see," O'Riley muttered. He picked a paper out of a stack

on the side of his desk and shoved it toward Seymour. "In the interests of full disclosure, counselor," he said.

Seymour scanned the documents, which constituted the medical examiner's report, items recovered from the scene listed by place of origin, scrapings from the victim's neck, her abdomen, her vagina.

"It's wonderful," he said, "how a human being becomes the repository for evidence, all classified from head to toe."

"An autopsy is much worse, organs slapped on a table, weighed, poked at." For once, O'Riley seemed to be voicing a straight thought.

Seymour ran his finger down the list.

"Well, in this case, an autopsy would have clarified some things. Like cause of death."

The prosecutor did not hesitate.

"In this game, we play the cards we are dealt. There was no way our Mr. Goode was going to sit still for an autopsy. Oh, we could have gotten one, but you know."

"Yes, I do, the clock is ticking, election less than a week away, and all those TV spots to be written and shot." He studied the prosecutor's face. "Speaking of time, you know, are you charging Junior or not? You can't hold him much more, or are you preparing his makeup?"

"One step at a time, counselor," O'Riley soothed. "I've just gotten this material, and as you have noted, regrettably, it's inconclusive in some respects. Semen removed from her seems to have come from two different individuals."

"Emily did get around. Even if it were only Junior's, it wouldn't prove much," Seymour responded.

"As long as it wasn't her husband's we have something. And we do have some hard stuff here. Cause of death appears to be strangulation, although the abdominal wounds cannot be ruled out. That, plus all the circumstantial stuff." He shoved a list of names in front of Seymour. "The start of a witness list," he said.

Seymour did not look at the paper.

"What's the tune we're dancing to O'Riley? Charge my man or let him walk."

"The tune, I'm afraid, is one you're not going to want to hear. We have, as you know in our custody, a Pedro Rivera who, we believed, killed a john, and this same Mr. Rivera, when apprehended, had in his possession a credit card belonging to one Seymour Lipp."

"Apparently Mr. Rivera gets around, too."

O'Riley smiled.

"As do you, apparently."

"You know that's a piece of fluff. There are a dozen ways he could have come into possession of a card I lost. With my wallet, weeks ago."

O'Riley's face hardened.

"You do know how fluff plays in the tabloids and on the tube."

"What is it exactly that you want?"

"That's better. Your client to negotiate. Quickly."

"Failing that?"

"We'll charge him with everything I can think of." The prosecutor's tone was flat.

"That's a crap shoot, and you know it. I can hold up DNA sampling of Junior for a long time."

O'Riley shrugged.

"I don't have too many other options at this point."

"Yes, you do, one more." Seymour pointed to the medical examiner's report. "You didn't mention the tissue under the broken fingernails."

"I didn't mention it because it doesn't match anything else found on the body."

"But I know what it does match to."

O'Riley's eyes widened.

"Haven't you guessed?" Seymour asked.

"Yes," he said. "And Rosenberg is on that one."

"Only problem," Seymour said, "is Mr. Gomez has an explanation."

O'Riley sat back in his chair as though contemplating an item he might purchase if the price were right.

"A good one?" he asked.

Seymour shrugged.

"I can't buy it absolutely."

O'Riley leaned forward.

"Maybe you won't have to," he said.

Seymour rummaged through the refrigerator and discovered a container of lo mein. He opened it up and smelled it, then he dumped it into a pot with a little water, and put it on a low heat. He lay down on the sofa, thinking that he would just close his eyes until the food was ready, but he awoke to Rosalie's lips on his forehead.

"Your dinner has melted into the pot," she said. "Anyway I've brought us some pizza." She took Seymour's hand.

"I haven't been able to find a trace of Lois, or the baby." She paused. "Well, that's not exactly true."

Seymour took her wrist and squeezed.

"Well," he demanded.

She stepped back, and now her eyes flashed.

"If it's so damned important to you, what's happened to her, why don't you track her down yourself. You must know how I feel about her, and this whole business. If it weren't for Junior, and the baby, I'd let her fall off the side of the earth. God, I'd even push her over the edge."

The blood rushed to his head, and he realized that not only was he angry that she would attack him, but he was also ashamed. His guilt rose in his throat, like a hot lump of half-digested food. What could he expect from her, after all. Was she Saint Rosalie? They were more than lovers. The strands of the knot that joined them twined through their lives. He knew that Junior and Lois loomed as dark shadows for both of them, but what he had not admitted, even to himself until this moment, was that Lois' shadow was more than a darkening screen. It called to him in the black reddened by lust. That is why he had sent Rosalie, with no concern for her feelings, to look after Lois. To protect himself. The lump in his throat coalesced, hard and bitter. He pulled Rosalie to him and embraced her.

"I'm sorry," he said.

"Then you do understand?"

"Yes."

"Okay, then," she said. "I believe you do. And I'll try again tomorrow."

"You don't have to. If it costs too much."

Her jaw set in determination.

"There's my niece. She's still an innocent. I'm doing it for her. Understand that. Not for you, or for us. For her."

He waited, but when she remained quiet, he asked.

"What did you find out?"

She shrugged.

"Like, I said, not much. The place was locked tight, curtains drawn. I asked the kids hanging out in front, but they didn't have anything to say. Except one. He smirked a little, muttered something about a dog, a very large dog. So I walked around the house, and I heard this thud against the back door, like it was going to be knocked off its hinges, and then the thing began to bark and growl, you know, the way guard dogs do. So I left."

"Let's work this mess out a step at a time," he said. "If I read O'Riley right, he's not going to charge your brother."

"He's going to go after Gomez?"

"I'm pretty sure."

She nodded, her eyes clear and determined.

"What's the problem, then? You can't believe that story he told you, that at the least you know is a lie, the part about Emily and you. Right?"

"Of course," he said.

"Then, if that's the case, let O'Riley do his job. And Junior will be out, your accounts will be squared, and we can move on. Together."

"Is it that easy?" he asked.

"No," she said, her eyes averted, "I wish it were."

After dinner, they sat at the kitchen table. Seymour sipped his coffee with one hand while drumming the table with the other. Rosalie's face was tight with a slight tremor on her lips She took his free hand to her breast.

"Maybe," she said, " we should just let it be."

He had had the same thought but he had dismissed the idea in the recognition that he was unable to state more than one simple fact of which he could be sure. He knew that Emily Levine was dead, but in his mind, Goode, O'Riley, and, of course, Junior, had become an unholy trinity, each pulling on a separate string that yanked him in a different direction. He wanted to rely on Rosalie as a fixed center among the disparate pressures, but her suggestion now unsettled him.

"I just can't do that," he said. "I didn't tell you before, but I stopped at my office before I came home, and I went down to the basement where I met the new night custodian. He showed me the spot on the floor where she lay, and he told me that his boss had told him to scrub that damned floor clean, but he said, somehow, no matter how hard he scrubbed the stains wouldn't come out. Now he just mops around that spot. Won't go near it."

Anger flashed on Rosalie's face.

"Has it occurred to you that everybody else seems more than willing to mop around that spot and to go on with their lives?"

"Sure, it has." He heard the tension in his voice and decided to let it pick his words. "The question is, are you one of those?"

"How can you think that?" She shifted her weight away from him. "What I'm saying is that we have our lives to think of. Together." She paused. "Don't we?"

He closed the distance between them, her words like a light in the darkness of his suspicion, but not strong enough to dispel all the shadows. It would have to be, he told himself, enough.

Rosalie had insisted that they try again to track down Lois and the baby. "We can agree on that, can't we?" she had demanded. "If nothing else, we have to try to find my niece."

However, when they stood in front of the house, their way into the alley leading to the basement apartment was blocked by a muscular teenager, one that Seymour recognized from previous visits. He had placed himself in their path, and a few of his younger brothers and sisters or friends stood behind him. They did not look like they intended to be moved.

"Let me try," Rosalie said. "At least I know his name."

"Martin, you remember me. I'm Rosalie Constantino. We just want to see how the baby is." She turned to Seymour. "You remembered the present, didn't you." She smiled at the teenager. "You know it's her birthday coming up soon."

"Don't be jivin' me. Her birthday don't come for two, three months. 'Sides, don't be callin' me no Martin. Folks 'round here be callin' me Hercules. You hear what I'm sayin'?"

"So much for the friendly approach," Rosalie whispered to Seymour.

"Okay, Hercules," Seymour said with a heavy emphasis on the middle syllable of the name, "now, let's try it a different way." He moved his body to within an inch of Hercules. He was a little taller than the teenager, and he stared down at him. "You got a problem with us walking around to the back?"

Hercules held his ground.

"No, I ain't got no problem," he drawled. "I'm lookin' at a man with a problem."

Seymour shifted his weight forward so that he pressed against Hercules' chest.

"I'm about out of patience," he said. "Now, we're going back, the easy way, or the hard way, doesn't make any difference to me, but it might to you."

Hercules' body stiffened and he pushed Seymour back.

"Now, don't be lookin' for no trouble. The lady said nobody goes back there."

"What's it your business?" Seymour growled.

"Maybe it ain't, and maybe it is, and maybe I do her a favor, and she be doin' Hercules, doin' him real good." He leered, and rubbed his crotch. Seymour exploded. He brought his knee up hard into Hercules' groin and then lowered his shoulders into him. The teenager staggered back, and while he was off balance Seymour grabbed him by the throat. Hercules started to struggle but Seymour increased the pressure.

"A little more and you'll stop breathing," he said.

"Back off, man, I don't mean you no hurt."

Seymour relaxed his grip on Hercules' throat and shoved him back so that he landed sitting on the top of a garbage pile.

"Don't says as I didn't warn you. Maybe the lady's busy. With your Daddy."

Seymour hurled himself at Hercules who scrambled to get off the pail. Before he could, Seymour took his shoulders and pushed down.

"You got a bad mouth, friend," he said. "Maybe you'd like to wear your balls for a bowtie."

Hercules contented himself with a scowl, and Seymour and Rosalie walked up the alley. The other kids separated slowly before them.

"She ain't home," Hercules called after them. "Ain't been home a couple of days. Just the damned dog howling, and the baby screamin'."

Seymour stared at Hercules for a second and then ran to the back of the house. Rosalie was a step behind him. He stopped when he reached the storm doors leading down to the basement. They were unlocked, and he threw them open. He started down the stairs and heard the dog growl and then thud against the lower door. He hurled himself against it and pain shot through his chest. He sat down on the bottom step and Rosalie crouched beside him.

"We're not going to get in that way," she said.

"You've got that one right."

"Are you alright?"

He rose to his feet.

"I think so, but we gotta get in there fast."

"What about a window?"

"Around the other side," he said.

They found the bedroom window that sat right at ground level. The dog apparently had followed their movement because now they could hear his claws scratching the wall beneath the window. Seymour stood so that he could kick the glass out.

"What about that beast?" Rosalie asked.

"After I break the window, you distract him," Seymour said.

"Terrific idea," she said. "Then what do I do?"

Seymour brought the sole of his shoe against the glass.

"I don't know," he said as the glass shattered, "but we'll think of something."

The dog's head appeared between the shards of glass, its teeth bared. Blood ran down its head. A piece of glass had lodged in one eye, and the dog, a german shepherd, was trying to throw himself through the window. As he did, he opened more cuts in his head. After a couple of seconds, he looked as though he had run into a propeller. Seymour saw a heavy board lying against the side of the house. He picked it up and brought it down as hard as he could on the dog's skull.

The dog froze for a second and then collapsed back into the room.

Seymour pushed out the remaining glass with the board, and motioned for Rosalie to wait. He sat down before the window and thrust his legs through the opening. He edged himself forward, grabbed the window frame, easing himself inside. While he was hanging suspended, he searched the floor for the dog. It was lying in a still heap just beneath him. He dug his heels into the wall, arched his body, and dropped into the room. As he fell, he realized that he wasn't going to clear the animal, so he split his legs and came down with one foot on either side of it. He lost his balance and broke his fall with his hands. He did not dare move. He thought he saw the dog's body quiver and he tensed, ready to roll to safety. When his leg muscles started to cramp, he lifted one foot over the body and twisted himself away. The dog lay motionless. He lit a match and in its light inspected the bloody head. The dog's mouth was ajar and its tongue lolled out between the fangs. Rosalie pounded on the door, and he blew out the match.

"Are you okay?" she said as soon as he let her in. "What about the dog? The baby?"

"The dog's dead, or if he's not, he's not going to be moving for a long time. Do you remember where the light switch is?" he asked.

He felt her pull away.

"No, don't you?"

He began to reply to the hard tone in her voice but instead he groped along the walls until he found it. He led her back to the bedroom. Rosalie glanced quickly at the dog and then turned away, surveying the rest of the room. "It doesn't look like anyone's been here for a while."

The bed was neatly made and the dresser top was clear except for a pocketbook standing on one side. One pair of shoes was in front of the closet. Seymour got up and opened the closet door. The clothes, mostly Lois', were hanging in place. He ran his hand over a black evening gown on one side of the closet and then a denim jacket on the other. He turned to Rosalie and shrugged.

"I believe the baby's room is down the hall," she said. "What did you expect to find in the closet, and why the hell are we dancing around in here when we want to find the kid?"

"Because," he said, "I don't think either of us wants to face what might be behind that door. But let's do it."

Rosalie opened the door, found the wall switch, and flicked the light on. The baby's room was tiny. It was dominated by a freshly painted white crib on one wall and an infant's dressing table on the other. A teddybear sat on a bentwood rocking chair in the corner next to the crib. Seymour took Rosalie's arm. He didn't know if she had seen the teeth marks on the top rail of the crib. The mattress was hidden by the bumper guard which had been shoved a few inches up against the bars.

"I see them," she said.

As if their legs were tied together, they each took a step toward the crib. It was empty. There was no sheet or cover on the mattress, which was pale blue except for a circular area in the middle that was much darker. Seymour reached in an felt the spot.

"It's damp," he said.

"As though it had been washed," Rosalie said.

"Do you think we should call the police?"

"No, not yet. First we can check the hospitals. But before that, let's see what our friend Hercules knows."

"He don't know nothin."

Seymour whirled to face the teenager, who was in the doorway. The belligerence was gone from his face, replaced by a shadow of concern, maybe even sorrow. He moved cautiously into the room, his hands extended in front of him.

"Peace," he said. "I'm sorry for that stuff outside, but you see you gotta understand that I'm the man 'round here, and I can't be lettin' no trash," he paused, "no trash walk over me."

"You could have saved us both a lot of trouble," Seymour said.

"Hey, man, what you bitchin' 'bout. I'm the one almost got hisself killed out there. Just to keep my face, you hear?"

"It is a pretty face," Seymour said.

"Now, don't be jivin' me." He turned to Rosalie. "You know what I'm sayin', don't you?"

"Sure," she said. "But you must know something."

He shook his head.

"Only this. That since her man in trouble, she been in and out, mostly out, and then she got herself that dog, mean sonofabitch, and told me, in front of my friends, you know, to keep everybody, I mean everybody, away from here while she out."

"And the baby?"

"I hear it cry sometimes, and then I guess it would get too sleepy, or maybe she be home and takin' care of her baby, but then, the last couple of days, I don't hear nothin' but that damned dog howling."

"And that's it?" Seymour pushed. "Nothing more."

"Like I said, I don't know nothin', and I don't want to be mixin' in no business that ain't mine."

Seymour steered Rosalie past Hercules and out the door. Seymour turned back to the teenager.

"Look, we're going out the front door. Lock up after us. Maybe you can fix that window."

Hercules' face soured.

"What I look like to you?"

"You look like a smart dude who wants to keep himself clean, who wouldn't want his customers to hear he got busted for dealin', very bad for business. So just do what I say."

Hercules's face softened into a grin.

"I hear you. But, hey what you want me to do with the dog?"

"Dump it someplace. You might want to bang him on the head one more time, you know, just to be sure."

They stood outside of the house in the grayness of a cold sunset. Rosalie's face was drawn.

"I should have tried harder," she said. "I let my spite for her get in the way."

"We don't know what happened."

"Don't baby me, Seymour, Jesus not now. That dog, those marks on the crib, and you know, when we checked, there wasn't a scrap of food in that house."

"I know," he said, "I know all of that."

"Then we sure as hell know what happened to that baby. So let's cut the crap and just find out the details."

$\triangledown$

Eight

ROSALIE'S HANDS SQUEEZED THE steering wheel, and her face was so ashen that her black hair and makeup against her white skin looked like a death mask.

Seymour did not know if she shared his suspicion that the baby might still be alive. Somehow, he had difficulty accepting her brutal death as true. In spite of the evidence of his eyes, his rational sense, fed by his recollection of Lois nursing her daughter, rebelled at such a horror of neglect.

He watched Rosalie's hands tightening on the wheel with each controlled heaving of her chest. He wanted to comfort her, to feel her close to him again. Either she had been more distant, or he had projected his own uncertainty on her, ever since she first expressed hesitancy about seeing Junior's case to the end. He wanted to narrow the gap, even if it meant pushing her to deal not only with the bizarre tragedy of the infant, but the mother as well, who was the cause.

"Do you think Lois could have done this?"

Rosalie drew her lips into a scowl, and her cheeks reddened with anger.

"You really, I mean, how can you ask me that?" Her voice crackled, her rage like static bending and distorting her words. She looked straight ahead, peering through the windshield into the black of the winter night. Her chest heaved beneath her heavy coat. After a moment, she took a deep, gasping breath. She dropped her hands from the wheel and turned to Seymour.

"Do you think I can have a drag?"

He handed her his cigarette and sought a way of easing the pain he had knowingly inflicted.

"It was unfair of me to ask that," he said. "I know you feel responsible for protecting Jennifer from her mother. And her father. But I don't believe this, any of it."

"You are a bastard, sometimes, you know. You're going to have to get this Lois business straight in your own head, and soon." The gentleness in her voice, though, undercut the edge so that he felt both soothed and attacked, as though she had cut his wrist with a surgically sharp knife and then applied her lips to the wound to staunch the blood.

"I know," he said. "I will."

"Should I take you home? You may be right, but I have to check. You know that. I can do it myself."

"No, I want to be there. And I don't want you to do it alone." She leaned over and kissed him.

"I need to go back in the house for a couple of minutes."

He thought he understood, and, in any case, his exhaustion lay too heavy on him for argument.

"I'll wait for you here," he managed to say. He closed his eyes and permitted his head to droop onto his chest while he waited.

He felt the rush of cold air and snapped his eyes open. Rosalie slid back into the driver's seat.

"Nothing here," she said.

He looked out the window and saw that they were parked in front of a local, private hospital. He sought the door handle and pushed it down, but she reached over and took his hand.

"Where are you going?"

He turned back to her and began to understand. He shook his head, hard, but he still felt as though he were looking at her through several layers of glass.

"You didn't have to do that."

"It would have taken twice the energy to wake you up. And besides I was pretty certain we wouldn't find anything here. A large anonymous place would be more her style, and even if she had been here, I didn't expect them to tell me."

"Which do you think it might have been, then?"

"She wasn't here. I'm sure of it. The administrator I spoke to looked at me like I was from Mars, and he wasn't that bright to be giving me a show."

"We'll try to the municipal hospital, and after that, whatever we find, we're going home. Right?"

He nodded, and she pressed the accelerator down until the car lurched forward.

They followed an ambulance into the emergency room entrance and waited behind the vehicle while paramedics threw open its doors. Their headlights shone into the ambulance and revealed a figure on a stretcher. The person's face was swathed in bandages, and a paramedic leaned over the inert body. It looked as though he were trying to trap the victim's life inside his chest by squeezing a wound closed. The paramedic in the ambulance stood up when the doors opened, but he kept his hands on the victim's chest until the stretcher was eased onto the ground. A doctor palpated the victim's throat and shook her head. The paramedic did not seem to understand. He gestured them to rush the body into the hospital. One of his colleagues had to pull him away. The others started to wheel the stretcher into the hospital. The body on it was small, a child of ten or twelve. The bandages on its face were soaked red, as were those covering its chest.

"I guess this is the place to come to if you want to blend in with the other disasters," Seymour said.

She began to speak, but instead opened her door.

"Let's get this business over, as soon as we can."

He reached across the seat to hold her for a moment.

"You don't have to, not this time."

"When are you going to understand that I must know. You stay here, if you want."

She freed herself and slid out of the car. Seymour caught up with her at the door to the emergency room.

A television set on the wall of the waiting room offered the late night news. The sound was barely audible, and nobody was looking at the screen. A couple of people thumbed through worn magazines, but it did not appear as though they saw the pages. In one corner, a plump young man in a straight jacket sat rocking quietly, a grin fixed on his face. His nose was flattened and swollen and a drop of blood oozed from one nostril. An orderly sitting next to him daubed at the young man's nose with a piece of gauze. The young man did not respond to the touch; he continued to rock. His tongue protruded from between his puffy lips.

Rosalie walked straight through this area to the desk. Seymour paused in front of the television screen, just in time to see Emily Levine's face disappear, and to hear an announcer indicate that the spot had been paid for by "Citizens for a Safer City." He recognized the name as a political action group for O'Riley's opponent. He stared at the screen, as though he could learn more, but the camera switched to the beaming features of the weatherman, standing in front of a map that showed a winter storm, brightly colored in blue, approaching from the west.

"I saw," Rosalie said. She was leaning on the desk, her head heavy between her hands. "But I don't want to deal with it, not now."

"What's going on here?"

Rosalie pointed toward a back office.

"We're waiting for somebody who has access to the records."

"Did the person you spoke to remember anything? It's not like we're asking about something that wouldn't stand out."

She looked over his shoulder and frowned. He followed her eyes to the stretcher passing behind them, the face of the child now covered and its arms folded on its chest. "Maybe, in this place," she said softly, "nothing seems important or remarkable."

A frail man, in his sixties, his face drawn and lined, emerged from the back office. He was carrying a thick file.

"The computer is down," he said. "I'd wish they'd just toss the darned thing. Most of the time when it's up, it's wrong, anyway." He smiled wearily. "If you're going to ask how I know it's wrong, it's simple." He placed his index finger to his forehead. "In thirty years, my memory has never failed me."

"Remarkable," Seymour murmured. "Do you then remember the case we're interested in."

The man's face broadened into a confident smile.

"Of course, but I will have to check the handwritten records. Fortunately, we still keep those. And there's always a first time, so we'd better check."

"I beg your pardon," Rosalie said.

"A first time," he repeated, and again pressed his finger to his forehead, "for this to fail." He thumbed through the pages inside the file. He stopped at one page, and drew his index finger over a line on it.

"Now what is your relationship?" he asked.

"I'm the baby's aunt," Rosalie said without hesitation. "Do you want to see some kind of identification?" She lifted her purse to the counter and opened it, but the man waved his hand.

"I don't think that will be necessary, under the circumstances."

Seymour felt his patience begin to falter.

"And those are?"

The man looked sharply at him.

"And you are? What is your interest in this matter?" He began to close the file. "You know," he said, "I thought I'd be helpful to you nice young folks, again especially in this case, but I don't have to do this. I could have you go through proper channels. And that could take, well, let's just say you're not going to want to wait that long because then you might have to come back when the computer is working."

Seymour bit down hard on his lip.

"Please excuse my husband," Rosalie said, her voice warm and reassuring, "it's just the strain you know. He's taken it harder than even I have."

"Now, of course I understand, and I see that I'd better make this as quick as possible." He reopened the file. "Two nights ago, yes, that was what it was, a young woman, gave the name, let's see," he peered more closely at the paper, drawing his nail over one spot, "name of, no, it's smudged." He looked up at Seymour and shrugged. "But the rest is clear. She brought in her child, said it had gotten caught between two animals that were fighting. The child was," he hesitated and lowered his voice, "I'm very sorry to say, D.O.A. There was absolutely nothing we could do."

Seymour saw Rosalie's face blanche, even as he felt his own legs buckle. He braced himself and drew Rosalie to him. She began to sob. The man closed the file and came out from behind the counter.

"Perhaps I can get you something?" he said.

Rosalie straightened herself.

"No, that's alright. We were prepared, but it's still a shock, to hear."

"You couldn't read the name?" Seymour asked.

"Why, yes, that's right. I can check again for you, if you like. But I'm quite sure."

"Yes, I know," Seymour said, pointing to his own forehead, "You've got even that locked in there. Did you see the infant yourself?"

"Oh, certainly not. It was all wrapped up in blankets."

"I see, but you do have locked in your memory, the child's age?"

"Of course, but let me check." He opened the file. "Yes, here it is, just as I thought, estimated age four or five."

Rosalie let out a small shriek and collapsed against Seymour.

"Is there anything wrong?" the man asked, confusion broad on his bony face. "She is the one you are looking for, isn't she? I'd hate to think, you know, well, it's impossible."

"No, she's not, thank God," Seymour managed to say. "But thank you for your time."

As he turned to leave, the man started to raise his finger to his head. "Sometimes—" he began to say, but then retreated into his office.

"Let me drive," Seymour said as they reached the car. "You can sleep if you want."

She handed him the keys.

"We're going home, aren't we?"

He shook his head.

"Look, I'll drop you off, but I've got a thought, and I have to check it out."

"You won't drop me off. If you have some crazy idea just because you saw Emily's face on the television, you'd better tell me about it."

He leaned against the car.

"I feel it coming together. This business with the baby. While we're here, something must be happening someplace else."

"Like what?" she asked.

The realization came to him.

"Something O'Riley said, when I talked about the evidence, and how I could prevent him from getting a sample from Junior, at least long enough to make charging Junior unattractive."

Rosalie shifted her eyes into the car for a moment, as though deciding whether she should drive.

"But maybe they can get something from Gomez, more easily," she said.

He nodded.

"Then, we'd better get there, don't you think?" She was quivering. "I know I can't stop you, and I'm not sure I would if I could."

"Meaning?" he asked.

"Just that. Nothing more."

They drove in silence as though they both recognized that whatever they found in Gomez' apartment, even nothing, would announce the end of the whole tangled affair. It occurred to Seymour, as they passed through the nearly deserted streets, that he was not prepared to conclude their joint efforts. Junior's problem had brought them back together after so many years, and even if he felt her tension as her brother's fate approached, they had formed a bond that he did not want to break. He glanced over at her sitting with her bright eyes fixed on the road ahead, her body erect and tense in spite of her exhaustion. The strong line of her nose, her expressive lips, the slender curve of her neck disappearing into the raised collar of her coat, all so familiar, saddened him. She seemed to feel his eyes on her.

"Anything the matter?" she asked.

"I guess I was just thinking about us. After this is all over," he said. He felt he had to be tentative. Too much was at stake.

"I've thought about that, too."

"And?"

"I don't know. I guess I'll deal with that one when we get there."

"But we will deal with it together, won't we?"

She smiled, her white teeth bright in the darkness of the car. His mood lightened with her smile. He had not realized how important the question had become for him. He felt comfortable enough to give voice to another thought that had struck him since they stood together staring into the empty crib.

"I've been thinking," he said, "that when all this is over I should fly out to the coast and look up my son. It's more than time."

Her face softened.

"If you want, I'll go with you."

"I think," Seymour said with a breath that seemed to expel a cloud of foul vapors, "that I would like that very much."

Rosalie turned to him.

"Do you think we could stop for a minute?" she asked.

He pulled the car to the curb. When he turned the key off, she put her hands gently on both sides of his face.

"We don't know what we'll find, or what we'll feel tonight, or tomorrow. So, let's just hold onto this moment for as long as we can."

He pressed his lips to hers and swallowed her next words in a long kiss.

Seymour parked a couple of blocks from the entrance to the complex of buildings that looked, in the moonlight, like so many shadowy obelisks rising high above the weary asphalt of the city streets. They got out of the car and walked briskly toward the entrance. When they were a block away, they could see two or three cars double parked. Several men were milling around the cars. Seymour peered toward them, and he was sure he could make out the outlines of the lights on each roof, but they were dark and still. They slowed their pace until they were about fifty yards from the cars, and then Seymour guided Rosalie toward the building line and into the shadows. They stepped over a low, iron post and rail fence that separated the sidewalk from a narrow area in front of the building intended to be landscaped with grass and shrubs but now a jumble of bottles, frozen paper bags, and newspapers. Seymour slid a cigarette out of his pack, and put it to his mouth. He felt Rosalie's hand on his, and he followed her eyes back to the cars. He thought he saw one of the men looking in their direction, and he took the cigarette from his lips. They flattened themselves against the building and waited.

For several minutes nothing happened. Seymour slid the cigarette back into the pack, and with his back pressed against the cold brick of the building, he edged closer to the cars. Rosalie followed, but then she held his arm.

"Do you think this is such a smart idea?" she whispered.

At first he was irritated by what was becoming a familiar refrain—as though she would take each step with him but heavily as a weight against his movement. But after a moment he recognized that her objection might be perfectly sensible.

"Smart has nothing to do with it. If we were smart, we wouldn't be here at all, pressing our butts against the wall. But I want to see the action."

She squeezed his arm instead of letting it go.

"Is that all?"

"Yes," he said, "probably that's all we'll do."

"That's not good enough."

"I know, but it's the best I can promise, right now."

They worked their way to the end of the building, within about thirty feet of the cars, which they could now see clearly were police cruisers. Although all their lights were out, Seymour could hear the soft crackle of their radios. Gomez' building was the next one, but a walkway separated them from it, and the path was, unfortunately, well lit. Seymour felt Rosalie nudge him from behind.

"What next?" she asked.

Seymour glanced over his head at the fire-escape ladder.

"Don't even think about it," she said.

"I wasn't," he said, although he had, for a moment, contemplated a leap from building to building. "I'll try to slip by and find a back entrance."

"And what should I do? Create a diversion by kicking over a garbage pail or something?" Her voice shook.

He held her hand.

"I want you to wait here, right where you are. In case they come out before I get up there."

She returned the pressure of his hand.

"Do you know what you're going to do?"

"No," he said. He loosened his grip and headed for the walkway. At the very end of the building a low hedge of scraggly yews provided some cover. He knelt down and eased himself onto his hands and knees. The ground was cold and hard. He could feel the rough, dead weeds between his fingers. He moved forward and carefully pushed a broken bottle aside. Within a minute, he was well down the walkway, past the point where the corner of Gomez' building screened him from the street. He stood up and flattened himself against the building. He could see a service entrance on the side of Gomez' building. Walking toward it, he felt exposed, although he knew he should be safe. He ran the last few steps to the entrance and started down the steps. His foot slipped on a soggy newspaper and he grabbed for the rail to steady himself. At the bottom of the steps, the door stood ajar, as he had expected, and he went in.

He paused to catch his breath in the stairwell on Gomez'

floor. His ribs now ached without pause, but he forced himself to the door leading to the corridor and cracked it open. He could see two uniformed officers waiting outside of Gomez' door, and he thought he could hear the low murmur of voices. One male voice rose now, and it was answered by two others, a man's and a woman's, speaking in Spanish.

The building was cool, but Seymour felt perspiration begin to trickle into his eyes. He swiped at it with the back of his hand and then pressed his ear closer to the opening. The voices were now fully raised, the men's harsh, the woman's a thin wail. Seymour peered down the hall just as a man hurled himself out of the apartment, knocking the two officers into each other. Gomez was dressed in pajamas and a robe. His feet were bare, and he was swinging his baseball bat at the officers. As one of them began to pull out his weapon, Gomez broke down the corridor toward the stairwell. Seymour flung open the door and stepped aside so that Gomez could run by. Seymour grabbed the bat and spun Gomez into the stairwell. He turned around to face the officers. Both of them had their weapons leveled at him. Gomez was frozen behind Seymour, his eyes wide, saliva dribbling from the corner of his mouth, his hands still clutching the bat.

Seymour fought an impulse to dive to the floor. Pain stabbed his chest. He thought he had been shot, and wondered why he had not heard the report. A man in a raincoat was now between the officers, a hand on each of the weapons, forcing them down. Out of the corner of his eye, Seymour saw Gomez launch himself down the stairs. Detective Rosenberg let the officers go and they charged Seymour. He could not will his legs to move, and they were on him in an instant. The first one to reach him was tall and powerfully built.

"Get the hell out of the way," he yelled, but Seymour

could still not move. "Fuck it," the cop spat and shoved Seymour aside. Seymour reeled and fell against the door he was still holding open. He looked down the stairs. Gomez had stopped on the landing below. His chest was heaving and he twisted his head to look up and down the stairs. The officer raised his weapon in both hands and aimed it at Gomez. Seymour started to grab for it but somebody pushed him down onto the floor. He looked up into Rosenberg's bloodshot eyes.

"Careful," Rosenberg said to the officer. "He's no use to us dead."

The officer cocked the hammer. Seymour struggled to get up, but then the shot went off and Gomez clutched his shoulder, dropped the bat, and fled down the stairs.

Rosenberg relaxed his hold on Seymour.

"Very good Jablonski. There's a commendation in this."

Seymour stood up slowly.

"Mr. Lipp," Rosenberg said, "you are awfully damned stubborn."

"I suppose you're going to say he resisted arrest," Seymour said between clenched teeth.

Rosenberg smiled.

"You saw what happened."

"I didn't see what went on in the apartment."

Rosenberg shrugged.

"It's of no importance."

"You have a warrant, of course," Seymour said.

"That's not important either, but yes, we do. Signed by the man himself."

Seymour felt the laugh well in his throat, but he bit down on his lip.

"Of course," he managed to say.

"You know," Rosenberg said. "I could have let them kill you."

"Why didn't you, then?"

Rosenberg shrugged again.

"Not because you're such a lovable guy, you can bet your ass on that. Let's just say it wasn't meant to be. And Mr. O'Riley, he don't like surprises."

Rosalie offered her shoulder to Seymour.

"There's no sense being proud," she said. "Just lean on me. And talk to me. I heard the shots and I expected to find you lying in a pool of blood."

"You weren't far off," Seymour said. He threw his arm over her shoulders and grabbed the iron bannister with the other.

"What's the hurry?" she demanded.

"Have to catch up with Gomez," he wheezed. He was finding it increasingly difficult to breathe.

"It's too late. As I was coming up, after I heard the shot, Gomez almost ran over me. As soon as I regained my balance, he was gone. Out the door. Into the waiting arms of the law. It was all very smooth."

Seymour noticed a splash of blood on her sleeve. She followed his eyes.

"Oh, I hadn't noticed." She moistened her fingers and started to dab at it, but he stopped her.

"That's what they were after. Evidence obtained in an arrest. Admissible," he said, "no fuss, no bother. Blood for DNA testing. This way the lawyers can't hold them up."

"Seymour," she said, her voice tinged with disgust, "don't you realize it's over. They've got their pigeon."

He let himself slide down onto a step. It was cold and his hand slid over the grime.

"Yes," he said. "I think I know that. But I can't stop until I know the truth."

"We can stop when Junior walks free," Rosalie said. "And out of our lives."

She sat down next to him.

"And then?" he asked.

"Then," she said slowly, confronting the realization, "I'll have to learn how to live with that."

He embraced her.

"We'll both have to live with that," he whispered, "'more than you can realize."

$\triangledown$

Nine

THIS TIME THE TELEPHONE worked, and Junior greeted
Seymour warmly. He looked fit; his blue denim shirt, clean
and starched, was stretched over his shoulders and biceps.
Curly black hair poked through his shirt, which was unbuttoned to the breastbone, and in the hair there sparkled a
thick gold chain. His smile radiated as though his body could
not contain his energy. It looked to Seymour as though
Junior could shatter the thick plate glass that separated
them as easily as if it were a thin sheet of ice, and walk out
shielded by the dense energy at the core of his being.

"Moving day, soon," Junior said.

"You've heard, then, about Gomez."

Junior's face glowed. He had to place his hand over his
mouth to restrain the laugh that would have brought a
guard.

"Heard? You gotta be kiddin'? The man is now in the cell
occupied by nobody else but Pedro, you know." He ran his
fingers of one hand over the knuckles of the other.

Seymour took a second to contemplate this intelligence,
to admire its audacious simplicity.

"I suppose he's sitting there with a notepad."

"He's wired, in case the poor bastard actually says something. But," he shrugged, "it don't make no difference what he says or if he don't say nothin', it all comes out the same way."

"I know," Seymour snapped. "Just a little bit more. To go with the blood sample they've matched with the skin under Emily's fingernails."

"Hey, the man blew it once, he ain't takin' no chances."

The smile crept into the corners of Junior's mouth again, and he began to hum the melody of "Summertime." Then in a surprisingly clear tenor he added the words, "Movin' day," he sang, "and the livin' is easy." Disgusted, Seymour slammed the telephone down, but Junior motioned for him to pick it up. The amusement had drained from his face, replaced by a blackening scowl.

"You know I'm walkin, soon. What am I gonna find?"

Seymour deflected the question.

"The world's pretty much like you left it. You'll probably have to find another job, though. The day after you were arrested, I received the court papers releasing you and me from each other."

"It ain't that easy, counselor, and you know it. Who gives a good fuck what the court says. You see how they operate." He paused, his neck muscles contracted and pulsing. "But they don't know, and what's more they don't care."

"Maybe they don't. But I do. We're even."

Junior shook his head slowly from side to side as if he were a priest hearing some remarkable blasphemy.

"No, no, my friend," he said, "not yet. There's Rosalie."

"What are you trying to hold onto?" Seymour demanded. "Your sister can make up her own mind, and I think she has. If there were any doubt, the theatrics with Jennifer did it."

Junior shrugged, his face impassive and blank.

"You must know all this," Seymour said, "but maybe hearing it will mean something to you. We tried to find Lois, but she has disappeared. We finally broke into your house and found a half-starved guard dog. When we didn't find the baby, just the dog, and signs of an attack, we checked the hospitals. One of them confirmed that such an infant was brought to them. Only it wasn't yours."

Junior drew his face back as though he had been slapped.

"Why, you bastard?" Seymour demanded, as guards approached from both sides of the partition. "Why the goddamned charade? With your baby. Your sister was already mourning her niece." A guard placed a hand on Seymour's shoulder, but he shook it off. "We're just about done," Seymour said. "Just a couple of minutes more, and you can have him."

Junior pressed closer to the glass, his eyes registering his anger.

"Hey, that was Lois' idea. Believe me man, I didn't know the details. She just said she would keep you busy. I didn't ask how. She knows you, remember, and she knows my sister. And anyway you were getting too close, man. I couldn't let you screw things up."

"And now you've got each other." He paused. "But you've lost your sister. And me."

"But you got her, right"

"Maybe not. You made her choose. And she couldn't."

"You two were fuckin' with my life." He banged his fist against the glass. "I did your time," he snarled, "I saved your pretty ass."

"We're even, now," Seymour said.

"Like hell we are. You didn't do shit for me."

Seymour watched while the guards wrested the phone from Junior's hand, hoisted him from his chair and led him away. Before they could get him completely turned around, he lunged back toward Seymour, his mouth still forming words Seymour could no longer hear.

Rosalie sat close to him.

"So, he admitted it? Said it was her idea?"

"Right. The baby is fine. And while we were prowling around the hospitals, they took Gomez. That was the whole point."

"But," she said, then paused while she looked away, "even for him."

"Yes," Seymour said, "even for him."

Rosalie glanced at her watch.

"Don't you want to see it?" she asked. "Somehow it seems right, that it's on television. Just like the beginning." She switched on the set.

Seymour reached over and turned down the volume.

"Tomorrow will be enough," he said. "If we're going to watch it let's do it this way. It'll make more sense."

And they watched O'Riley, tweed hat just a little tilted, and pipe at first clenched between his teeth. Seymour noted the practiced timing, the way the pipe moved in and out of the prosecutor's mouth in counterpoint to his words. The camera shifted to Gomez, his arm in a sling, walking between two detectives. His eyes were as wide and staring as Seymour remembered them on the stairs of his apartment building. Microphones were thrust in his face, and he snapped at them like a dog worried by taunting children. Finally, a well-dressed man intruded and moved his lips in a brief sentence. Then the picture cut to the beaming face of Pedro. Seymour turned the sound up in time to hear a voice-over intone praise for the brave convict who at the risk of his life, reported the confession of the depraved murderer. As the video returned to O'Riley, Rosalie leaned over and turned the television off. Seymour saw tears streaming down her face.

"I wasn't going to tell you until," she swiped at the tears, "until, I don't know, maybe never, but I just can't stand it any more."

Seymour suddenly remembered what had been bothering him.

"When you went back into the house, you found something, didn't you? I was asleep, but I seem to remember something. And you have been on the other side of a very long bridge since then."

She nodded.

"You know then," but he could not bring himself to express his thought.

"No, I don't know, not for sure. But I found this. She reached over to pick up her purse from the end table. She opened it and slid out a belt. "This, I found this outside in the yard, beneath a stone, a hiding place only he and I knew about, since we were kids. It was there, neatly folded."

"Almost as if," he said softly, "he half expected you to find it."

She shrugged, and he picked up the belt, scraping off the dirt that encrusted it. He saw the holes where the studs used to be.

"I saw him wearing this, that first time, when Lois came for me."

"And not since?"

"Not recently. You should have told me, you know. Before," he said, anger rising in him. "That is more important than anything else."

"I know," she said softly. "I betrayed our trust. It's as hard as that. And I did so because I thought I wanted him free. At any cost."

"And now?"

"Now, I realize that although I cannot tolerate the thought of him in prison, possibly for the rest of his life, I am more terrified that I might lose you. And if you gave me a gun with which to shoot him, and if shooting him would stop you from leaving me, I would pull the trigger."

He started to reach for her, but let his arm drop to his side.

"It's too soon," he said.

"I know. But maybe one day, it won't be too late."

She spent the night in her own apartment, by unspoken agreement between them. When he awakened, he reached to the other side of the bed expecting to feel the still warm imprint of her body but the sheet was cold. He waited to hear the water run in the sink but when it didn't he sank back against the pillow. So many mornings he had enjoyed watching her dress before he himself got out of bed. Even now, he could remember how a tangle would catch in her brush, and she would pause to run her hand through it while his nerve endings joined with hers, so that it was as though he were guiding the thin wrist and long, graceful fingers in a gentle tug that freed the hair before the long sweep of the brush.

"Am I such a show?" she would ask, and turn back to the mirror to run her hand in a nervous gesture over the spot where the tangle had been. He would nod, and now lying in his empty bed he tried to explain this feeling to himself, but the thought resisted words, refusing like the tremulous shape of a cloud that offers the earthbound observer a new face with each gust to settle into a distinct and steady form. He started to rise from the bed, still holding a last image of her as she sat in the chair, her leg crossed over her knee, her skirt tight against the swell of her stomach and the inside of her lean thigh, taut as she pushed her shoe on.

He stood next to her on the fringe of the crowd of reporters. They had spoken briefly in the morning when he arranged to pick her up, but they had said little to each other, as if unable to deal with the shock of their sudden estrangement.

O'Riley had called just as Seymour was leaving to ask if he and Rosalie would participate in the news conference. When Seymour had said that they wouldn't, O'Riley had tried to insist, saying that at least Seymour's presence was

necessary to complete the "symmetry" of the scene. Seymour had let the prosecutor's smooth voice flow over him
while he removed himself from any contact with it.

Even though it was a warm morning for late winter, Lois
was bundled in an ermine coat. Her face was carefully made
up with decorous strokes of blush and a matronly soft red
lipstick, and her thick black hair had been tamed into gentle
waves that lapped the collar of her coat. She glowed with a
false healthiness that matched the superficial warmth of the
air. When she stretched her hand down to her child who
tottered between her and Junior on the steps of the courthouse, she uncovered the unadorned flesh of her wrist above
her white leather glove, and it had a sickly pallor.

The child's face beamed up happily at her parents. She
held onto Junior's hand and amused herself by swinging
back and forth at arm's length. She wore a white fur coat to
match her mother's, and Seymour could see a black scuff
mark on her freshly polished white shoes. She threw herself
into an arc that brought her against Junior's leg, and she
laughed as her father leaned down to pick her up. He, too,
had been refurbished for the occasion in a dark blue business
suit and a tan raincoat that he held folded over his arm.

Seymour watched Lois. She seemed unsteady, her body
rocking almost imperceptibly on her high heels.

"She's stoned," Seymour murmured, but Rosalie did not
respond. Seymour could not be sure who held her eyes so
intensely, but he guessed it was Junior. He scanned the
group. The rage he had felt when he had first seen the
reunited Constantino family now began to dissipate. He
permitted a smile to curl the corner of his lips. The tableau
was so ridiculous in every detail: O'Riley's cap far back on
his head while he punctuated every sentence with a stab of
his pipe, looking like a bizarre hybrid, part Sherlock Holmes
and part Madison Avenue executive; Junior's pagan energy
unnaturally forced into the conservative blue suit, with Lois

struggling to retain her balance and dignity, probably wearing, Seymour thought, pink shorts cut to her crotch beneath the ostentatious ermine; and, of course, the centerpiece, the toddler child raised from the dead like Lazarus. All of them, posturing to the assembled press, struck Seymour as too ludicrous to warrant his anger. Not even Goode hovering behind them in transparently false modesty, occasionally casting a furtive eye at his coat on Lois' back, could rekindle the rage.

"Looks like everybody is happy but us," Seymour said to Rosalie. This time she turned to him for a moment, and he could see her eyes both moist and coldly hard.

He felt a surge of hilarity rise to his head.

"Gomez will be shipped off to a funny farm," he said as an irresistible laugh gripped his throat. "O'Riley serves Junior, Lois, and baby to the adoring media, and to all the good citizens who can now sleep more soundly knowing that the bold public servant was right all along." He struggled to choke the laugh so that he could finish. Rosalie's frame had started to tremble, but an exorcism, he thought, is an exorcism, however it occurs. "And Goode's honor is preserved, clothing the whore and addict who is now his surrogate daughter." The rage boiled up again, suddenly, and convulsed in a hacking fit that prevented him from giving voice to the howl he wanted to hurl at them all.

"He's guilty," Rosalie said, her vehemence surprising Seymour.

"We don't know that," he began and then recognized the reflex. A cameraman, apparently bored with O'Riley's performance, turned toward them, and Seymour wheeled them around so that only his back would provide a subject for the lens.

"I know that," he whispered at last. "But I also know that I love you. The rest of this," he waved his arm back toward the press conference, "doesn't matter. I have to go on with my life."

He was about to progress from "I" to "you" to "we," but when he looked into her face, he saw that her eyes were closed against it. Instead, he withdrew a piece of paper from his pocket and handed it to her.

"I'm leaving tonight, on this flight," he said.

She glanced at the paper, folded it up, and slid it into her purse.

Sleep swallowed him that afternoon, its offer of oblivion far more inviting than anything consciousness could provide. He awoke in the early evening and looked out of the window of his apartment at the black sky, blank but for one distant star. He reached for the telephone, and held it in his hand until it began to hum loudly. He placed it back on its cradle, then picked it up and dialed the number of a limousine service.

The area next to the boarding gate held a handful of people sitting, it seemed to Seymour, as far away from the next person as they could.

Seymour had bought a newspaper, which he opened to the front page. He scanned a story until he reached the bottom of the page where it requested the reader to find the continuation, and then he laid the paper on the seat next to him. He looked, for the hundredth time, down the corridor that led to the waiting area, and for a moment he thought he saw her hurrying toward him, but the woman turned and disappeared into another corridor.

He saw that an elderly couple across from him was staring at his newspaper. He brought it over to them.

"I'm finished with it," he said. "Why don't you read it, if you like."

The woman looked nervously at her husband.

"Why, thank you," he said. His smile revealed ill-fitting and yellowed false teeth. "Don't know when that darned plane'll get here."

Seymour looked out the window at the blinking lights and bulky shape of a plane rolling toward the gate. On the ground it looked, he thought, as graceless as a pterodactyl.

He heard the loud speaker crackle and a shuffling movement began among the passengers. As he reached into his coat pocket for his ticket, he felt a hand squeeze his arm, and the pressure sent a surge of warmth into his belly. He turned and saw her smile.

"I hear the surf is up in Malibou," she said,

"So it is," he aid. "And it damn well better stay up until we get there."

They walked together through the tunnel. Seymour stopped her for a moment before the door to the plane. The night was bright with moon and stars, and Seymour imagined he could hear the ocean, only a few miles away, crash its powerful rhythms against the shadowy sand. He waited a moment longer, as though the words he wanted to say to her would form from the foam of the surf, in the ancient echo, or perhaps they would emerge in the dark sky where he envisioned the circles of the gulls whose harsh cries he could almost hear as a tremulous counterpoint to the waves.

"I feel," he said slowly, hearing his voice swallowed by the roar of the engine, "that it is right for us to be here. Together."

"And?" Rosalie whispered into his ear.

"And that we have a chance."

He saw the starlight catch the white of her smile.

"That," she said, "is all that we can ask for."